STAY
NORTH

STAY NORTH

NORTH

A NOVELLA

SHELLI ROTTSCHAFER

Shelli Rottschafer

2021

atmosphere press

Without question there are places in nature that own a certain unique spirit, that are so peculiar and individual that they draw us to them, not that they care, but that they stand out in the surrounding solitude and vastness of the forest and act as magnets to anyone who passes their way.

- Jim Harrison, *Sundog* 59

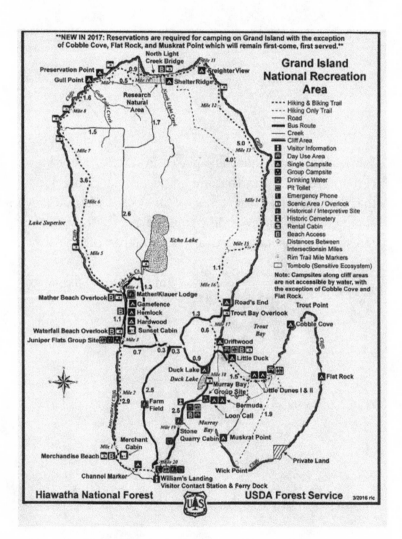

NEW IN 2017: Reservations are required for camping on Grand Island with the exception of Cobble Cove, Flat Rock, and Muskrat Point which will remain first-come, first served.

Grand Island National Recreation Area

- - - - Hiking & Biking Trail
- - - - Hiking Only Trail
——— Road
——— Bus Route
——— Creek
▬▬▬ Cliff Area
Visitor Information
Day Use Area
Single Campsite
Group Campsite
Drinking Water
Pit Toilet
Emergency Phone
Scenic Area / Overlook
Historical / Interpretive Site
Historic Cemetery
Rental Cabin
Beach Access
Distances Between Intersections in Miles
Rim Trail Mile Markers
Tombolo (Sensitive Ecosystem)

Note: Campsites along cliff areas are not accessible by water, with the exception of Cobble Cove and Flat Rock.

North Light Creek Bridge
Preservation Point
Gull Point
Freighter View
Shelter Ridge
Research Natural Area
Lake Superior
Echo Lake
Mather Beach Overlook
Mather/Klauer Lodge
Gamefence
Hemlock
Hardwood
Sunset Cabin
Waterfall Beach Overlook
Juniper Flats Group Site
Road's End
Trout Bay Overlook
Trout Point
Cobble Cove
Driftwood
Trout Bay
Little Duck
Duck Lake
Flat Rock
Murray Bay Group Site
Little Dunes I & II
Farm Field
Bermuda
Loon Call
Murray Bay
Stone Quarry Cabin
Muskrat Point
Merchant Cabin
Merchandise Beach
Private Land
Channel Marker
Wick Point
William's Landing
Visitor Contact Station & Ferry Dock

Hiawatha National Forest

USDA Forest Service   3/2016 rlc

The Arrival

Noelle

Noelle leaned her forehead against the passenger window speckled with rain drops. She and Harrison had just rolled down the drive and pulled into the parking lot of the municipal ferry to Grand Island. Offshore, in the distance, rose the island. Its trees waving their green leaves like an open hand in greeting.

Her husband, Harry, exits the Suburban and rounds a puddle as he approaches the pay station to confirm their noon reservation on the pontoon ferry to the island. There are few other cars in the lot. The daily tourist traffic has slowed due to the rain showers.

Noelle could see shadows of Harrison and whomever he was talking to within. Some people sat in rocking chairs on the front porch. Mountain bikes lined the asphalt below, waiting to be selected by forthcoming tourists.

It had rained the whole four hours of their drive north. They had left this morning from their home in Boyne City, crossed the Mackinac Bridge, and now were stalled at the ferry parking lot on the west side of Munising. It was a long ride, full of silent contemplation for both of them. Noelle and Harry were on what could unravel as their final trip together. Their therapist had suggested this "Divorce-moon" as their last chance to figure things out, before they filed their papers in court.

Noelle waits in the humid vehicle. Reaching for a piece of gum in her bag, she narrates the scene before her; "Eighteen years of 'bliss' all to be determined by a rainy weekend at a rustic cabin. Welcome to beautiful Grand Island in Lake Superior just off the shores of Pictured Rocks." Her voice sounds like a radio announcement for a "Pure Michigan" ad campaign.

While Noelle watches the shadowbox outline of Harrison in the pay station, she notices a couple in heated conversation and observes, "looks like we aren't the only ones not enjoying each other's company."

A barrel-chested man sits, gesticulating his arms. His movements rock him back and forth on the chair. A seated woman turns toward him as she buries her face into open palms. She seems to be weeping.

Martin

Martin and Elena sit on the edge of paired rocking chairs. Their yellow raincoats drip and water pools around their feet. Moments before, they had unloaded from the ferry. Now, Elena admonishes Martin as he looks toward the parking lot for his clients' arrival.

"Martin, you said this trip would be your last of the season. It's time to go home."

"Elena, I'm not ready. If we go back, we have to deal

with all the shit that is there. That's why we left in the first place."

"Why we left? No, why *you* left Marty."

"Come on Elena. You know all of this. Detroit still hasn't recovered economically. I'm not inspired in a big city. I am a Nature Writer, damn it. I write about the outdoors. Places in the woods. There is very, *VERY* little of that there."

"Martin, I followed you here after you went back to school. I was perfectly fine where I was, but not without you."

"So, what are you complaining about? You found your own niche. Traverse City isn't that far away from Marquette. We rendezvous in Mac City. That's three hours for me with crossing the bridge and paying tolls in comparison to your two-hour drive north. That's a snap."

"Always the martyred starving artist. For fuck sake, I am tired of this distance Marty."

"Listen, I finish with these clients in less than a week. When I'm done, I'll close up the cabin on the island, and store my stuff in my apartment in Marquette. Then I'll be down to TC. We can discuss it more once I'm there."

"Discuss, yah sure. Yet again, another one of your soliloquies. You realize I am your audience, right? The discussion will be between us, and not just a monologue in your head, Martin."

"Why are you so angry? It's not as if you have been doing nothing and twiddling your thumbs. Elena, you have a year left in your program at NMC. Why the hurry?"

"Back in Detroit I had a good job. I was a wine steward. I have already studied enough. I have my Level One. I was practicing what I learned. What I am doing now is a waste of my time."

"But with your knowledge from your sommelier classes and the program at NMC, we can move anywhere. We could go to Lake Tahoe, Telluride, Park City. You can work for one of the high-end restaurants at a resort. I will start my own excursion business. I can write, I will have plenty of material to inspire me out there. What's the problem?"

"So you are willing to move forward but on *your* terms. Why West? What's so wrong with Detroit, where we have family? Martin, I am tired of waiting for you. I'm tired of the excuses. I have learned all I am going to learn at NMC. I could leave and finish my degree online. I could leave, and with what I already know, get a job pouring wine. I want to go back to Detroit."

"Frankly, no one is stopping you, Elena. Go."

"Excellent. Your response is for me to just go. Go on my own?"

"Yes, Elena, go if that is what you want."

"Martin, you ask me why I am so angry. You haven't noticed. You aren't getting it. I am late, Martin."

"Late for what? Late for finishing your Associates from a local community college? This is just the cream on top. It will get you where you want to go. I thought that was what I was doing with getting my M.F.A. but my path diverged."

"Yah, alright, Mr. Robert Frost... that worked out *really* well. Instead of being the next great Ernest Hemingway or Jim Harrison, you are leading rich white people on glamping trips."

"F-ing hell, Elena. Who do you think we would be catering to back home? It's the same clientele, different fucking city."

"Whatever. Talk about white flight. It's just as bad up here. Martin, the Upper Peninsula has like 1% of black people. Racism is here, too. Even if there is a smaller population and therefore less encounters of it, you can't escape race in the great North Woods. Besides, you are ignoring what I said to you."

"Cut the crap, Elena. What are you bitching about now?"

"Don't talk to me that way. You started with the negative spiral, I wasn't going there. I was having a fine time until you got into it about how horrible home is."

"I don't see why you want to go back there so badly, before you finish, and before I close ties here."

"You still aren't getting it. Apparently I have to be super blunt. Marty, I am three months late with my period. I took a home pregnancy test that I bought at the grocery store in Munising. I used it in the outhouse while waiting for the ferry before I got onto the island. It was positive."

"What? You have known this whole time we've been on the island together but didn't tell me until now, when I am about to pick up clients?"

"I wanted the right moment to tell you. It didn't arrive. Now, I have no choice but to tell you. To me, it is happy news. Obviously, you have a different opinion."

"How am I supposed to react minutes before you leave and I have to put on the 'happy host face' for my clients?

"All I know is that tomorrow, once I am back in Traverse City, I am going to Planned Parenthood for a checkup. I am pregnant, Martin. I am pregnant with *our* baby."

"We've talked about this. Elena, kids aren't an option."

"A child is not an option. It is a reality, Martin. Grow up."

"I am not ready to be a dad to anyone."

"But you are. You are now."

"You have to take care of this, Elena."

"What do you mean? Are you kidding me, Marty?"

"I'm not ready."

"You are fucking thirty-three years old. What is it? Do you think you are going to save the world at thirty-three like Jesus-fucking-Christ did? It's time to act like an adult, man. What are you waiting for?"

"Elena, it's an awfully simple operation. It's not really an operation at all. They go in with a vacuum."

Elena stared at him in disbelief.

"It is surprising how little you know about the medical world or how it relates to a woman's body. Do you not get it? I have passed my first trimester, Martin. The baby has a heartbeat. Our child is forming into a living being. I want to be a mother. I am older than you. I don't know when I will have another chance. Being thirty-five puts me at higher risk just because of my age."

"I would go with you. I'll stay with you the whole time."

"You aren't even listening to me. You are only hearing what you want to hear. This isn't a one-sided conversation."

"It takes less than an hour and then it's all perfectly natural."

"How do you know how long it takes? And natural, what the fuck?"

"Plenty of women lose a child. Plenty of women have abortions. It's not our time, Elena."

"I would consider it if I were younger. I would consider it if I was not in a committed relationship. I would consider it if it would get in the way of my future, my profession, my convictions. But this child, *our* child, will not."

"We'll be fine afterward, if only you will get the procedure. We will be just like we were before, Elena."

"What makes you think so, Marty? If we are arguing over this now, how will it be better afterward?"

"It's the only thing that bothers us, planning for an unknown future and one back in Detroit, at that. It's the only thing that makes us unhappy. It's the only thing we ever argue about. I am not ready to be a father. I am not ready to go home. Can't you understand?"

"Yet, Martin, what you aren't hearing is that I'm ready to be a mother to our child."

"You don't have to be afraid. I've known lots of people that have done it."

"Done it? Had a baby or had an abortion? I also know plenty of people that have done either. What are you saying, Marty?"

"Well, if you don't want to, you don't have to. I wouldn't have you do it if you didn't want to, Elena."

"What are you talking about, man? You were just moments ago trying to convince me to have the procedure. Is this some reverse psychology bullshit that you are trying to work on me?"

"We could have everything, if only you could wait, Elena."

"We can have everything, and we don't have to wait, Marty. We can go home. We can have a home. We can have careers. You can start a business. You can write. I will be a sommelier at a nice restaurant or open a wine shop. We can start our family, together."

"No. Absolutely not. We can't if we go back to Detroit.

It may be where we are from, but it is no longer home. Not for me Elena. It isn't ours anymore."

"It is too ours, Martin, if we make it ours. It doesn't have to be the Detroit of the 1960s with the race riots. It doesn't have to be the Detroit of the 1980s, all bombed out. Detroit is rising. We can create our own resurgence. But, if we let other people define for us what Detroit is, if they take away our peace. If we take away the possibility of having this child, then yes. We will never get it back."

"Maybe. Let's wait. We'll see."

"So, you are willing to reconsider, Martin?"

"I don't want you to do anything you don't want to do, Elena."

"Martin, you've got to realize. I don't want anybody but you. I don't want anyone else. I'd do anything for you."

Martin stands and the rocking chair hits the back of his calves as he steps away in exasperation. "Damn," he sighs.

Martin stopped his conversation with Elena because a man exited the pay station. The stranger turned, offering an outstretched hand.

"Martin? With Grand Island Outfitters?"

"Yes, I am Marty Rouge. Are you Mr. Phillips?"

"Call me Harry." Pointing to the car, he gestures. "My wife, Noelle, is over there. We are your guests for the next few days." Noelle exits the Suburban and her long legs carry her to the group.

As the three await her approach, it is clear that Harrison had interrupted an argument. The pair attempt to wipe away their intense expressions and swap them for strained smiles.

"Mrs. Phillips, I'm Marty. This is Elena Díaz." They all

shake hands.

"Hi, I'm Martin's girlfriend. You will love Grand Island. I was out to the cabin for the past week. We have been getting it ready for you both."

"Oh, you aren't staying?" inquires Noelle.

"No, I live in Traverse City. I'm finishing my culinary degree at Northwestern Michigan College."

"I love TC. I have some college friends who now live there," replies Noelle.

"It's been a change from home, that's for sure. We're Detroiters. We met at Wayne State for our undergrad. Culinary school will be my second degree. Marty is up at Northern Michigan finishing his Masters."

"Marty, whatcha studying at Northern?" asks Harrison.

"Creative Writing. Nature Writing to be exact, so nonfiction."

"How do you two like it 'Up North'? Do you miss being down-state?" wonders Noelle.

"I prefer it up here. Marquette is a little small, but you can't beat the sunsets over Lake Superior."

"Marty, you are one of the last real romantics it seems. How about you Elena?"

"Well, Mrs. Phillips, it's not home. It's surely not home. I'm from Southwest Detroit, or what some people call Mexicantown. Marty is originally from Hamtramck. Up here. Well, let's just say it's different. Different than what I'm used to." Elena grabs her backpack and swings the strap over her shoulder. "I'll be off then. Nice to meet you both."

Elena steps toward her car and beeps the alarm. She opens the passenger door and tosses her bag on the seat.

Rounding the hood, she yells, "See ya, Marty."

Meanwhile, the three raise their hands in goodbye.

Harrison

Harrison had agreed to this long weekend because "Up North" was his happy place. Ever since he was a kid, Harry had come to the Upper Peninsula, so, he figured the stay north would be the best place to try once again with Noelle. He wanted things to be different than what had happened with his first wife. He was willing to work on their relationship but he resented the fact that the therapist was calling this their "Divorce-moon". He felt that name was setting up the weekend for inevitable failure.

To calm his nerves before the trip, Harry reread some passages from Jim Harrison for inspiration. Perhaps the philandering JH wasn't the best choice, but he was Harrison's favorite author. Originally from northern Michigan, JH writes of his love for the land and how this connection impacts him. Similarly, Harry is drawn to these northern woods. Perhaps even like Jim Harrison, they are his one true love.

For the weekend, Harry tucked JH's novel *Sundog* into his duffle bag. When they loaded onto the ferry to cross the channel to Grand Island, Harry was reminded of one of the author's points. There are some places on earth that stand out. These places act as a magnetic force that pull certain people together and create a connection between them and nature. Michigan's Upper Peninsula is one of Harry's magnets. It seems to reset his personal barometer every time he is up here. When the therapist planted the seed for a getaway and Noelle agreed, Harry started looking for ways to come back north, once again.

Harry called his duck hunting buddies to see if they could suggest any outfitters that catered to excursions in the UP. Lars, Harrison's buddy who had bought into a duck camp near Munuscong on the east side of the peninsula, suggested "Grand Island Outfitters." Since Harry's knee replacement surgery, Lars knew his friend would prefer a glamping-style excursion. Long gone were their primitive camping adventures during college. Back then, a two-person pup tent, freeze-dried meals warmed on a camp stove, and shitting in the woods seemed like heaven. Twenty-plus-years later, both Lars and Harrison had matured to expect the comforts of deluxe-sized beds, meals made to order, and plenty of alcohol to numb the aches earned during the day.

Grand Island Outfitters seemed the perfect fit. The company offered a few options depending on budget and desire. One could opt for primitive camping, stopping at a backpacking site each day. A mid-range option reserved rustic cabins along the trail, which could be accessed through a hike-in or rental mountain bikes at the ferry dock pay station. The final option, the one that caught Harrison's eye, were the private log cabins on Trout Bay near the Little Duck and Dunes I and II campsites.

Harrison and Noelle would have a day to acclimate to the camp along the white sand beach. A second day of fishing would close with a relaxing bonfire. A third morning mountain bike ride, followed by a late afternoon of skeet shooting, would culminate with a final feast to clear out the cupboards. On departure day, after morning brunch, the couple and their guide would head back on the noon ferry to mainland.

It seemed like the perfect plan for a beautiful long weekend; one that could instigate a rejuvenation or the demise to Harrison and Noelle's eighteen-year relation-ship. As he boarded the pontoon ferry, Harrison thought, "I am not sure what I want more, an end or a new beginning."

In the Beginning

Noelle

In the beginning Harrison created heaven on earth. He provided the adventure. He splurged on every occasion. He embodied what Noelle's mother had told her she should want in a husband. Noelle was naïve back then.

As always, first encounters leave lasting impressions, and Noelle's initial encounter with Harrison surely did that. It was subtle, but his glance sparked an inner fire. All humans know this feeling. It's that connection when the eyes meet and the gut reacts. When it happens, it is magical.

For Noelle, it all began at a soccer match. The referee tweeted his whistle and the game commenced. A tall man with greying temples ran past her cutting toward the left-hand goal post. Noelle didn't know him, but he had her team's orange and royal blue jersey blazing across his chest.

Noelle dribbled the soccer ball down the center, anticipating a shot. The opposing team's center halfback lunged forward to try to steal the ball just as she righted it to the tall man posting left at the goal. 'Tall Man' connected to the ball and left-footed it into the goal, while the opposing center halfback had too much momentum and plowed into Noelle. Her feet slipped from under her. She landed on her ass hard and knew she would have a bruised tailbone from the smack down. The tall man approached and extended his right hand to her right forearm lifting Noelle to her feet.

"Nice assist," he smiled.

'Tall Man' was Harrison, and that is how Noelle's eighteen years of slumber started. He was the lord of their household. He protected, and provided, and did what he had been raised to do. He was completing his obligations as the great provider, or so he thought. In his mind, he fulfilled the social contract he agreed upon throughout their marriage. He had completed his side of the bargain.

The truth of the matter is that Harry acts through a feigned parental disposition, and not merely for Mathias and Malachi, their two boys, but for Noelle, too. It seems as if Harrison thinks she is the eldest child. And often like a first-born, the two bump heads in what he perceives as Noelle's rebellion.

All Noelle can say is that after eighteen years, she tires of it. Noelle tells him she is tired of the belittling. Tired of him talking through her while she speaks. Tired of the condescending. Tired of the arguments. Noelle attempts to explain to him that the way he treats her is not right. By exemplifying this to their sons, he is teaching them that this is normal behavior. Noelle and Harrison are showing Mathias and Malachi that the way Harry talks to her is the way they should approach their future partners. Harrison sees no problem in this. It is his normal.

Noelle has sought help from her therapist. The therapist's response is that if Noelle wants change, she must create it. If Noelle wants the relationship to evolve, she needs to initiate it, because Harrison believes everything is as it should be. If Noelle wants progress, then she needs to train Harry and her boys. Instead, she realizes, Harrison has trained her into uncompliant submission. He has educated the boys how to treat her, and any other woman.

The therapist suggests a 'Divorce-moon' to initiate reconciliation or a demise. If the two of them really are at the point of rupture, then they need to take time to assess. The kids can safely relax at their grandparents' house while Harry and Noelle negotiate if this relationship is worth saving. Harry thinks that their relationship can survive simply because he doesn't want to go through a second divorce. He has failed once before, and doesn't intend on doing so again. Noelle hopes for their marriage, because that is what she does, hope. Hence they are here, in the Upper Peninsula hauling coolers of food, baggage filled with gear, and hiking boots onto the pontoon ferry to Grand Island.

The Phillips, Martin, and other tourists board the ferry. Crossing over the choppy water of Munising Bay, Noelle realizes she is out of her element. Harrison has the advantage as the outdoorsman. He is in his comfort zone. She is not.

The spray from the bow hitting the waves causes Noelle to shelter behind Harrison's shoulder. With an apologetic smile Martin asks the pair, "You been up here before?"

Harry nods. "To the Upper Peninsula, yes. Not to Grand Island."

"How did you hear about Grand Island Outfitters?"

"My friend Lars recommended the company. I guess he has been out here before? He scouted out places all over the UP before he decided to chip in to a property on the East side."

"Right, I forgot about that... Lars Thompson."

Noelle observes the exchange between their guide and her husband. As the launch pulls into the landing, she's not sure if she likes how this is starting. Will Marty be Harrison's good-old-boy? Will she feel the odd-one-out merely for lacking a Y chromosome? Or is it a fact, that no matter where you are, and where you run, your problems follow?

Martin

Martin realizes his head is not where it needs to be after Elena's disclosure. His brain is in a fuzz. He is lost in his own thoughts rather than being able to make small talk with his clients.

His mind keeps returning to the fact that, "we... she, is pregnant." How the hell is Martin supposed to deal with Elena's admission while working and watching over these new people?

Harrison and Noelle Phillips are Marty's last excursion of the season. Perhaps they will be his last clients altogether if Elena gets her way and Detroit beckons. Martin feels embarrassed because while Harry was inside the pay station, Noelle observed Elena's emotional ultimatums. He wonders what Noelle overheard or how well she can read lips. Yet, he shrugs it off for the moment. Noelle and Harrison seem like a pair with their own complications. There is a silent tension that is palpable even to those who first meet them.

Martin checks his mental address book that he and Harry have a mutual acquaintance. Lars Thompson is a good guy. He has been out to the island before with some of his buddies and their hunting dogs. Lars's descriptions over the phone helped Martin assess what to expect over this last long weekend in July.

Lars described Harry Phillips III as a fifty-two year-old, twice married Trust-afarian. Standing six foot five, his rounded shoulders hide a once athletic build. Martin looks upon Harry, then glances at Noelle while the ferry hands tie the boat to the pilings. He wonders what she sees in him now that Harrison is weighted with a potbelly. Martin presumes this will be yet another boondoggle. Predictably, the couple will succumb to the numbing indulgences of evening cocktails, remark on the beauty of the deciduous forests, and lull themselves to sleep with the waves along Lake Superior. Martin knows firsthand how nature can heal, but will she?

Harry seems like one of Martin's usual clients, bored middle-aged men looking to re-encounter their lost youth. Lars had confessed to Martin that Harrison really does not need to work due to his inheritance but continues to log hours "at the office." Harry's furrowed brow doesn't conceal his disdain for his underappreciative wife nor his obligations to their two wild teenage boys.

In Martin's quick judgement, Harrison seems like he would open up more lofting a bourbon during a fireside conversation. Whereas Noelle was a bit of a mystery. A decade younger than Harry and a decade older than Marty, her Botox-brow creates a façade that Martin can't decipher. Noelle seems to be in a struggle of wills because her demeanor demonstrates she has not embraced her "Soccer Mom" status. Marty guesses she would rather be traveling the world, imagining she is carefree, not wanting the reality of her years or presumed loyalty to dictate her behavior with Harrison.

Upon arrival, the service dock at William's Landing on Grand Island is bustling. Martin waits for the other tourists, mountain bikers, and day hikers to unload before he sets the Phillips's baggage and cooler on the worn wooden planks. Marty stretches his right hand across the water and Noelle grasps it to leap in one bound to the dock. Harrison follows with his own long-legged step and bends to sling his duffle over his right shoulder. Noelle extends the handle on the cooler to trail it behind her. Martin shoulders her bag and leads them to the parked ATV in the shade of the Grand Island Visitor Center.

Harry climbs into the passenger side with his duffle over his lap. Noelle sits in the back, facing outward with her legs dangling over the cooler. Her duffle rests at her left on the back cushion. Marty twists the key left in the ignition and turns the ATV onto the graveled path that winds four miles toward their destination, the log cabin on Trout Bay.

Martin drives slowly along the route to stop at points of interest. The threesome pass cottages once owned by the Cleveland Cliffs Iron Company executives. Marty explains to Noelle and Harry the local history. "Some of these houses are still maintained as summer residences, but most are empty. The US Forest Service purchased the entire island and incorporated it into the Hiawatha National Forest. Once the last descendant passes, these places will return to the earth. One day it will look pristine, like it was meant to be."

At the Stone Quarry Log Cabin historical site, Harrison reads an interpretive sign. "One of the oldest standing structures on Grand Island, the cabin was built around 1846." Noelle trails off absentmindedly as Harry murmurs behind her. She walks out on a granite slab covered by ankle-deep water coming into shore from the bay. The chill of the lake sends goosebumps across her skin. While she uses her hand like a visor, Noelle watches the sightseeing boats make their way east toward Pictured Rocks National Lakeshore.

Martin calls them both back and they load onto the ATV. A mile and a quarter down the dirt road from William's Landing, the three linger briefly at the island old timers' cemetery. Because the mosquitos are thick, the group only pauses to read some of the names on the tombstones. "Desjardins, Hawkins, Powell. Hey, Harrison, no Phillips here," teases Noelle. Martin listens to her banter and wonders if there is a hidden hope in her morbid joke.

Further on, the three wave hellos from the vehicle toward a boat anchored off the Murray Bay Group Campground picnic site. Children swim in the shallows. On shore, a man guards a grill with a spatula in hand. Nearby, a woman straightens a red-checkered piece of fabric across a picnic table. The watermelon centerpiece and upside-down plates anchor the corners of the cloth in the gently blowing breeze.

Smelling hamburgers and hotdogs charbroiling, Harry audibly hopes, "Are we well stocked with some good grub for tonight? I ,for one, am feeling a grumbling. How 'bout you guys?"

"No worries. We'll eat well this weekend," replies Martin. "Tonight we can barbeque some chicken and there are plenty of veggies for a salad."

"Well, hammer it down then," quips Noelle. With her prod to go faster, Marty slides the ATV into gear on a stretch of two-track. The hardwoods above merge into white pines and tunnel the three toward the cabin.

A quarter hour later, Martin pulls into the drive of the log home. "Welcome. This is our cabin; it is one of a few private homes on the island. Everything else is maintained by the US Forest Service." Martin parks and they all step down from the vehicle.

"How many people go through Grand Island Outfitters"? asks Noelle.

"We try to run an excursion every other weekend throughout the summer. The ferry operates from Memorial Day to the first week of October, but we usually close down Labor Day weekend. It gives me a chance to either recuperate at my apartment in Marquette or go down to TC to visit Elena before school starts."

"That's a full summer season," affirms Harrison.

"True, but this year, the owner is shutting down excursions after your trip so that he can bring his family up here for part of August."

"I see. So, there aren't many people on the island then. Is it mostly day trippers?" wonders Noelle.

"Right, some people come out to mountain bike for the day. Then again, there are some researchers. On the north end are the Bio-Research areas. University of Michigan and Northern Michigan send students out there periodically."

Martin holds the front door open for Harrison and Noelle, "Home Sweet Home, at least for a few days."

The Phillips walk over the braided rug in the foyer to the living room. Opening eastward toward Trout Bay, a picture window frames the dune grass and water in the distance. Below the window stands the dining room table, and the kitchen continues to the right. They pause at a glass-cased armoire housing a full liquor cabinet. Harry reads the labels.

"You are finishing your Masters at Northern, Martin? You will have to tell us about it. We are trying to encourage our oldest, Mathias, to look into that school." Noelle steps into the kitchen as the men hover at the doorway.

"You chose to go to school there? What on earth are you studying that you couldn't have back in Detroit at Wayne State?" asks Harry in disbelief.

Martin opens the cabinet for Harrison so he doesn't have to squint through the glass. "Well, my girlfriend, Elena, is bewildered by that same question. I did finish at Wayne State. Yet, because of the economy in 2008, I was part of the exodus. I stuck it out for a while, but a degree in English is a hard sell in the business community of downtown Detroit. I tried to pull it together but that rat race wasn't working for me."

Harry pretends to listen but his thirst over rules him. He grabs a bottle of Mount Gay rum and walks into the kitchen looking for a cola in the fridge. "So, you got out of Detroit and headed north. Not a bad decision. I wouldn't mind doing that myself. Getting outta dodge, that is."

"I wanted to follow my dream," vocalizes Martin.

Noelle peers into the refrigerator behind Harry and spots her requested wine coolers. Speaking into the cooled cavern instead of at Martin she absently comments, "I think we all need to follow what the Universe calls us to do. What's your passion, then, Marty?"

Martin takes the rum and coke Harrison pours for him and admits, "I want to be a writer. I know I am going to be a great writer, one day. Elena thinks I have these grandiose ideas, but I am nearly there, I can feel it."

Harry sits down at the head of the dining room table. He holds court, sipping his drink, while Noelle and Martin prepare the evening meal.

"Do you read Ernest Hemingway or Jim Harrison? Is that why you came to northern Michigan? That Harrison is a genius. Pun intended," Harry says pointing at himself with a smile.

"Ah, so clever, Harrison. Like-minded kindred spirits attract new people to the tribe. Have you found your tribe in Marquette, Marty?" wonders Noelle.

Martin bastes the chicken with barbeque sauce. Noelle chops romaine lettuce for a salad. She hands Harrison a paper sack and a cellophane bag filled with ears of corn. It's his task to shuck the cobs.

Marty continues. "Of course, who up here hasn't read Jim Harrison? And no, community has been hard to find. As you can tell, I am a little older than the average student at Northern."

"I imagine it's hard to enter into a community that is already well established," affirms Noelle.

"When I was accepted for my M.F.A., I was intending on working with a well-published author who was Chair."

"Oh yah? There's another Jim Harrison in our midst? I've been meaning to begin a new read. Who is he?" asks Harry.

"Smolens is his name. His reputation is what drew me here. I was hoping he would be my mentor. Yet, the cohort before mine was his last. Right when I was accepted, he retired."

"Damn the luck, how do you feel about that?" sympathizes Noelle.

"I decided to go forward with the program anyway. Elena was super frustrated. She still is... for a variety of reasons. You may have picked up on that at the pay station when we were saying our goodbyes."

"Women can usually find a problem in any little thing. Don't listen to 'em." Harry winks in collusion.

"Be quiet, Harrison! Marty, you *should* ignore my husband. Women are perceptive. Perhaps Elena is seeing something more to the situation than you are allowing yourself." Noelle enunciates this with a chop of her knife.

"Maybe Elena simply is sick of being here. Not here, here, because she is in Traverse City, but here as in a state of being. Elena is thirty-five, two years older than me. She wants to go back to Detroit to start a family. She thinks we have accomplished all that we can up north. She believes that it is time to return home." Martin toasts his statement with his glass lofted in the air. "To home, wherever that may be."

"Yet, you don't think so?" Noelle wouldn't let his attempt to end the subject slide.

"I am not ready to move back. I don't know if there will ever be a Mrs. Rouge. I like my freedom. I am not ready, and I am never going back to Detroit."

"Never say never, my lad. Women can be pretty convincing," affirms Harrison.

"While you are up here, finishing your degree and

working for the outfitter, what does Elena do?" Noelle was back at it, defending the sisterhood she was creating with an unknown woman.

"Elena finished her Bachelors in Hospitality Management at Wayne State. Now she is studying for her Sommelier Certification. Since she began, she has passed her Level One."

"Is she in Traverse City to gain more knowledge as a vintner? We have friends who are part of a winery and tasting room. It's called Left Foot Charley. Have you been there Marty? Harrison, we should put Elena in contact with them."

"Noelle, please. Quit being such a busy body. If Elena has spent any time in TC, I'm sure she has been to Left Foot Charley," retorts Harry.

"Elena isn't in upper Michigan to merely go wine tasting, or so she reminds me. She studies at Northwestern Michigan College in their culinary program. Really, though, she came up north to follow me. She gave up a lot. But I think we have gained plenty by coming here too."

"I take it Elena doesn't really like it up north?" Noelle queries.

"She's homesick. For the life of me, I don't understand why she can't adjust."

"What's the draw down state for Elena? Why does she want to go home?" asks Noelle.

"Because her family is still there. She comes from the Latino side of town; her family is enormous. She misses them. Also, she feels like she is doing nothing. She says she is wasting her time. I beg to differ. She has made connections. She is learning. NMC has plenty to offer. Last Fall she took two classes, "Today's Hospitality Industry" and

"Principals of Marketing." She needs to stay current with the trends. She'll have to know that stuff wherever she goes."

"What did she think of those classes? You see that she learned something, does she feel the same?" Harrison voices this, because he worries for his son. If Mathias began college, would he embrace what his professors were teaching? Would he be open to learning? Would he retain what he had learned? As a defiant child, with poor grades, and a struggling attention span due to ADHD, Harrison wonders if his son could cope in higher education.

"She has learned the most from her internship. Last Spring she interned at 2Lads Winery on Old Mission Peninsula."

"Sure, I know it. They have decent reds there," affirms Noelle.

Martin nods. "This upcoming Fall, she is transitioning into a Manager Position at 2Lads. She will pour in their tasting room, and will continue on with her final class at NMC."

"What is she planning on taking? I for one wouldn't mind learning more kitchen techniques. I get sick of making the same food for a household of growing boys."

"Her class is called "World Cuisine." It teaches ethnic cooking. It will be good for Elena to know how to make a wide variety of meals. I mean, she can make some seriously good posole and green chile enchiladas straight from her *abuela's* recipes. But, she needs a wider range, more than just from her own heritage."

"So is her goal to open her own farm-to-table restaurant and pair wines with dishes?" asks Harry.

"That's what I would like to see her do eventually. But

in the meantime, I don't see why she is griping about following me. She most assuredly is gaining something from being up here." Shaking his head in bewilderment, Martin places the bowl of salad on the dining room table. "Let's change subjects. A toast, to the moon rise and what this weekend may bring."

Over an hour later, once the evening dishes were set aside and the carnage of barbeque chicken laid in the trash, Martin scavenged the recycle bin for a set of empties. With Founders All Day IPA cans in hand, he exits the cabin to set them on the fence beyond the porch railing leading to the beach path. Then he returns to his room to unlock the gun safe and extract two 12-gauge shotguns.

Martin had deduced during the dinner conversation that Harry was a decent shot. Previously, he had come north to hunt for duck on the east side of the peninsula with Lars and their other buddies. Noelle was another matter. Listening to her ideas about everything's interconnectedness to the Universe, Martin doubts if she would want to be included in an impromptu target practice.

After having deposited the smelly supper remnants in the bear container out on the two-track gravel road, Noelle comes into sight. She wrings her hands and wipes them on the thighs of her shorts to dry her fingertips. Marty's eyes linger a little too long over Noelle's body as she approaches. At forty-something, she still is a good-looking woman.

From conversations over dinner, Martin gathers that Harry owns his own business. Meanwhile, Noelle devotes herself to their two adolescent boys, who at this stage feel they no longer need her. Yet, she dedicates her days to bringing them to soccer practice, yelling at tennis referees during matches, or dropping the boys off at the movies as their friends hover in the lobby. It's apparent that Noelle relishes something different to occupy her daily itinerary.

Martin loads the two chambered over-under 12-gauge with target loads and sets it on the picnic table on the porch. Then he slides three shells into the chamber of the other auto-loading 12-gauge and asks, "Hey, Noelle, do you want to shoot off a few rounds with Harry and me? We are far enough away from other campers and cabins so they won't call the authorities to complain."

Noelle walks up and grabs the shotgun from the picnic table. She backs away from the porch rail, primes the pump, and eyes the cans lined up on the fence before the dune grass. She holds the shotgun with her left hand, and puts her right index finger onto the trigger. She levels the muzzle, plants the butt in the crook between her chest and shoulder bone, and points in the direction of the first can. A loud bang floats in the air, her left arm rises as she steps back from the blow to her right shoulder.

Martin hoots in surprise. The can flies into the air and lands a few feet behind the fence in the sand.

"Right on Noelle, nice shot! Looks like you've done this before."

Noelle shrugs off his compliment. "Harrison belongs to a gun club. Sometimes we take the boys out there for target practice or clay pigeons."

"You don't back away from the force of the shot. You've learned to move with the pull."

"Thanks. Never in my life did I think I would like holding a gun or shooting at something. But I do. It's nice to feel in control of something." Noelle looks at Harrison as she says this, but he ignores her words.

"Well, if you like shooting skeet, tomorrow after dinner we can go over to the old lodge. The neighbors, two college guys who are volunteering with Historic Construction of Michigan, are housed there for the summer since they're refurbishing the Mather Lodge. They have a thrower and we can take a few shots if we bring dinner to complement their stock pile of tequila."

"Sounds like a plan!" Noelle states with a high-five, and hands Marty the gun with her other hand.

Harrison

Harrison listened to Martin and Noelle's planning for the next day and thought, "Lars did me right. This guy, Marty, seems like he knows what he's doing. He entertains Noelle and provides enough rum to keep me humming. It'll do."

Cocktail in hand, Harry strolls out of the cabin to the beach. At the end of the trail through the dune grass, four plastic chairs stand like a totem pole, one stacked on top of each other. Further down toward the shoreline, where the sand is still soft and not wet from the lulling waves, there are remnants of an old bonfire. Harrison turns right to walk the beach looking for driftwood. As he spots a stick, he tucks it under his left arm. Gradually, his bundle grows and he cradles it back to the pit. As he begins spiraling the logs into a small teepee, Noelle joins him on the beach.

Under one arm Noelle has a Pendleton blanket. In her other hand, she grasps two metal rods, one side is a poker, the other a wooden handle. She sets the blanket on one plastic Adirondack chair and leans the pokers against the other. Noelle unfolds the blanket to reveal a white plastic grocery bag containing a box of graham crackers, a packet of Hersey's Chocolate bars with almonds, and a sack of marshmallows.

"Look what I found in the broom closet. Fancy sticks for s'mores. No need to find branches and file off a pointy end with your jackknife. Cool, huh?"

From bended knees, Harry rises to look in her direction. "I don't feel like eating anymore. This is my dessert." He raises his rum and coke to toast her.

"Oh, come on, Harrison. One s'more won't kill ya."

Harry turns to grab some dried dune grass and sticks it under the teepee of driftwood. He flicks his lighter and singes his fingers while Noelle punches a hole in the marshmallow sack. She draws out two cubes and spears them on a metal poker. Harry blows on the smoldering grass and the driftwood catches fire.

"The stars are beginning to twinkle through the haze. Do you think there's going to be a full moon tonight?" asks Noelle.

"We'll see the moon, but it's not full. If we're lucky, we'll see some aurora borealis. Up here it looks like a fluorescent green mist that dances over the horizon, but they can be red and purple in color, too."

"You mean Northern Lights?"

Harrison nods in recognition, watching Noelle burn her first two marshmallows.

"Damn, I got too close to the fire and they went up in flames." She flings the tip of the poker downward to launch the charred goo into the fire. Noelle steps back to the plastic chair, and places two more marshmallows on the stick to try again.

"Wait a few minutes. Let some of the driftwood break down into ash. Use the ash and coals to toast the marshmallows golden so you don't burn them again."

"You know everything don't you. Perfect marshmallow toasting techniques."

"Knock it off, Noelle." Harry demands from one of the plastic chairs.

"But you do. You know everything. Is it fun being a know-it-all?" Noelle leans back on her heels, her knees point toward the fire, the Pendleton blanket drapes around her back.

"What's really the matter, Noelle? We came up here because your therapist suggested we get away from our usual routines that bog us down. What don't you like now?"

"It isn't fun anymore. Not any of it. I feel as though everything has shriveled up inside of me. I don't know what to say. I don't know how to explain it. I don't know if I want to try to explain it. Maybe this is what the Universe is trying to tell me. Maybe it's telling me 'don't analyze it Noelle, just let it be'."

"Isn't love fun?" Harrison tires of Noelle invoking the Universe. He'd rather her be grounded in reality.

"Oh, shut up, Harry." Noelle turns to place her now gold marshmallows on a graham cracker that's adorned with a segment of chocolate. She puts the poker between her knees to hold it. Sandwiching the oozing marshmallows, she slides them off the poker between her long index finger and thumb.

"Here's a poker if you want to roast some, Harrison. I am going to walk down the beach."

"Alright." Harry watches her take a bite of the s'more, and then wipe the leftover ooze on her pant leg. The light of the fire lights her back as she fades into the dark, camouflaged by her dark jeans and black fleece top. "Do you want me to wait for you to come back, Noelle?"

"You don't need to. I'll be able to see where to go by the moon shadow."

Harry ponders in silence. Looking out over Trout Bay, a green mist reflects off the water on the horizon.

A Day In

Noelle

Noelle is the first to rise. It's a practice she has developed in order to have some meditative time before Mathias and Malachi wake. Noelle claims sunrise for herself. Careful to not rustle the bed too much, she swings her legs to the floor and stands. Harrison gently snores, curled around his second pillow. Martin is also awake. She hears his shower pelting like rain.

Noelle takes her journal from the nightstand. She walks through the darkened cabin, shoulders the Pendleton blanket on the couch, and steps onto the deck. The bay opens eastward and the sun is awakening in the distance. She sits on the first step leading down to the beach. Noelle extends her legs into a seated fold stretch, and draws the blanket up around her. Rising, she takes in a deep breath to begin her day. The smells of yesterday's campfire and the morning dew coming off the dune grass mingle. Her memory clouds with last night's conversation with Harrison.

Leaving that ruined moment behind, Noelle steps toward the cabin. It is breakfast time.

Inside, she searches for the kitchen lights. Flicking them on, she begins opening cupboards to find the coffee, creamer, and sugar. She can hear the men, both beginning their morning routines. Noelle opens the refrigerator and takes out an onion, green pepper, a sack of potatoes, and a dozen eggs. From the microwave used as a bread box, she untwists the tie from a package of English muffins. She lays all of this on the counter to prepare breakfast, but stalls for a little music.

Noelle powers on her cell to the Pandora station. She is happily surprised that the connection reaches this remotely on the island. The signal bounces over from the satellite in Munising. At odd moments, the music grows silent as the phone displays the channel reloading. Yet, a song fills the spacious cavity of the kitchen. Eddie Vedder's voice croons. His song, "A Better Man" tells of a woman who settles for a life without love. The words are her practiced goodbye speech which the she never utters. Rather, the wife is stopped by convention, or her complacency. She chooses to pretend. She fakes sleep. Caught in her own depression, she is unable to get out of bed in the morning.

Yet that immobility, is not Noelle. In response, she mutters under her breath, "What the fuck is this?" Vedder's lyrics sting. Could "it" be said that easily? If Harry walked into the kitchen now, would she finally have the courage to tell him, once and for all, that it was over?

The woman in the song dreams of other possibilities. But, in the meantime, continues her lie. She tells the man she loves him, her words ring hollow. She is too afraid to end the comforts of her relationship and begin anew. The song taunts Noelle.

Last night, as she and Harry laid in bed. The hum of

the mosquitoes floated by their heads and she whispered, "I love you, Harrison." He rolled on his side. With his back to her, Harry grunted in response. Her lips, puckered for a last kiss, lingered unmet in the air. So entrenched in their usual roles, he didn't feel she needed the same validation. But he was wrong. Everyone needs to hear that they are loved, are worthy, are cherished. Perhaps Harrison could feel her words were a farce. She was saying them just to say them and to see what his reaction would be.

Noelle rests her brow against the kitchen cupboard. She takes in the silence as the song finishes. Her internal dialogue acknowledges that at one time, she had loved Harrison. She knows that she doesn't want to leave her relationship this way, with it being her decision to pull out. She doesn't want to be the one to file for divorce, because honestly, if she did, she would be leaving so much behind. Harry and the boys would condemn her as breaking up the family. It would be her fault.

Harrison walks into the kitchen. From the drying rack next to the sink, Harry palms a pint glass and opens the refrigerator for the jug of orange juice. Placing the glass and the jug on the counter, he turns to the liquor cabinet, and reaches for the bottle of Mount Gay rum. "What? I'm on vacation," he justifies.

Noelle lifts her head from its resting spot against the cupboard, her hands remain busy chopping onions on the cutting board. Tears stream down from her face.

"What now, Noelle? Why the tears?" Although his words could sound like he cared if spoken with empathy, Harrison's tone is indifferent. He is tired of her emotional highs and lows. Tired of the drama created out of nothing.

"Nothing," oddly resonating his own last thought. Noelle assures in an unconvincing voice, "It's just the onions. I am going to make cottage fries and a veggie hash with a fried egg on top."

Yet, Noelle knows, it is not nothing. Her tears are not from the onions, but from knowing she would stay. Pretending everything was alright, she would feed Harrison and Martin their first meal of the day, just like she did every other day for Mathias and Malachi.

Noelle's silence avoids the truth. She continues the cycle she has created for herself. In an attempt to cover up her real emotions and to sidetrack Harrison's attention, she asks, "Hey, Marty, what kind of eggs do you like, fried or scrambled?"

Martin

The cleaned breakfast dishes drain in the drying rack. Noelle busies herself in the guest room and gathers her things for a day on the beach while the men try their luck at fishing on the bay. As Martin and Harrison head out the screen porch door, Martin explains, "In the old days Trout Bay was an Ojibway summer camp. Local bands would travel along the Lake Superior coast. During harvest they would haul in whitefish or lake trout, and smoke the catch to preserve the meat. In late July, the women would pick thimbleberries or wild blueberries to dry. They stored pine needles for medicinal tea. And, the birch trees could be stripped of their bark to repair canoes or reinforce wigwams."

Marty and Harrison slide one of the aluminum row

boats off its station by the dune grass. The two men use arm strength and thigh muscles to rest the sides of the boat. They waddle their way down the grass, to the inclined beach, and ease the hull into the shallows. Harrison swings the bow out toward the bay and holds the stern. Martin fetches the cooler of sandwiches and drinks, placing them in the bow on the floor. He runs ashore to grab their poles, the net, and the live basket to hold their catch.

Martin tips the boat slightly to port as Harrison holds on. Marty crawls to the middle and eases out the oars to help balance the boat while Harrison lifts his long legs over the railings.

"See where the cabins are now? That was where the natives had their summer village. This bay acts as a natural harborage. The cedars beyond the dune grass berm protect from the winds off the bay. Behind the trees, past the ATV trail, are blueberry patches. This would have been the perfect camp way back when."

"Do you ever find arrowheads or anything like that?"

"I haven't. But interesting things come ashore with the flotsam. Beach glass, old shards of china, plenty of driftwood. Nothing from back then. More than likely, if you are doing new construction on the island that requires excavation, you will dig something up from the mining days. The executives from the Cleveland Cliffs Iron Company used to have their summer cabins out here."

Martin rows past the cabin along the right-hand side of the bay out toward the cliffs that make the tombolo, or thumb shaped peninsula of Grand Island. The two men slowly edge their way to the point. Marty's breathing intensifies as he rows. Harrison ties lures and casts the lines out behind the boat. They troll along the edge of the bank where the bottom drops off suddenly. No longer near the sandy bottom, the water deepens but is clear. The shadow of the trees and bursts of intermittent sunlight play with the sandstone precipices.

"The fish aren't striking," complains Harrison.

"True. It's a little late. We are midmorning. The lake trout usually bite early. We would need to go deeper and drop downriggers. The trout hang out where the warm water meets the cold."

Harrison loves to fish. He fishes with his boys that is how they connect. So fishing now, with Martin seems like a small betrayal to Mathias and Malachi who are back down state in Boyne City with their grandma.

"My sons would love it up here. Maybe next year we'll do a boys trip."

Beside the boat, on the shaded side closest to the shore, a big trout surfaces. Martin hears the splash of its tail and pulls hard on one oar so that the boat turns and the lure glides past where the trout was feeding.

"They're nibbling the mayfly debris on top of the water," notes Harry.

"Unfortunately, I doubt they'll strike the lure," says Martin. "Let's cross the bay, and once we get there we can pull ashore for a lunch break."

The wind tunnels through the mouth of the bay and helps Marty push toward the shore with his oar strokes. Harry's poles fruitlessly remain in the water as he grabs a cold Molson can out of the cooler. "It's noon somewhere, right Marty?"

The two men continue in silence. The comradery of men needs no words, just a shared activity. Martin labors to move the boat across the bay. Harrison lounges with his feet on the seat, his back against the starboard side, and the poles in their keepers trail uselessly behind him.

As they near the shore, the nose of the boat skims a sand bar. Harrison reels in the poles and Martin jumps into the shallows, guiding the boat into shore. Harry swings his legs over the port and lowers himself into the thigh deep water. Together, they pull the boat up the beach. Martin lifts the cooler and Harrison grabs the boat cushions for them to sit on. Marty places the cooler between them, opening it to find ham and cheese sandwiches bound in cellophane and waterproofed in a Ziploc baggy. Harrison drives his hand into the ice to pull out two more Molsons.

They position themselves on the beach, on the left-hand side of the shoreline toward Trout Bay Lookout. From their spot, Harrison watches fancy color-shirted mountain bikers peer across the bay on a break from their morning ride. In the other direction, across the bay, are the few privately owned cabins. Noelle's red square beach towel beacons in the distance.

"Why didn't Noelle come fishing?" asks Martin.

Little waves lap at the stern of the row boat lodging the nose into the sand. Harrison chews his sandwich and swigs from his can. "She needs some down time I suppose."

"What's the matter, Harry? You guys have been together for how long?"

"Eighteen years. I don't really know what's wrong, or what is going on in Noelle's mind. But I never do with the women in my life."

"So this isn't your first rodeo? I suppose none of us has it perfect, myself included."

Harrison shakes his head, "We're going to a therapist. Noelle has changed quite a bit since we first met. Back then, she loved to party. Now that we have kids, Noelle 'is searching for a newer path,' or so she claims."

"Are you included in that path?"

"Excellent question. I think she is bored. Bored with her life. Bored with me. And instead of rising to the challenge of that boredom, she wants to break up something that was once good."

"Or, at least *you* thought was good."

"Yah, maybe. Noelle's therapist suggested we go on a trip to concentrate on 'us' away from other distractions. I suggested the Upper Peninsula, and Lars, my buddy, told me about Grand Island Outfitters. That's how we chose to come here."

"It's a good place to get away from things, but I don't know that the island provides the answers. Only you can do that."

Harrison finishes his sandwich and balls up the cellophane, dropping it into the baggy. He gulps down the last bit of his beer. Rising to his feet, he dusts the sand off his thighs and puts the boat cushion back in the hull of the boat.

"Do you mind if I walk the beach back, Marty? It'll be a lighter load for you anyway with your rowing."

"Nah, that's fine. Just help me push the boat out into deeper water."

Martin throws his empty can and all of the wrappers into the cooler, and lofts it into the bow. Both he and Harrison grab a side of the boat and slide it into the water. Marty swings his legs over the rail as Harrison holds the other side for balance. Martin puts the oars into the water while Harrison shoves the boat toward deeper water.

Marty matches the pace of his oars to Harrison's progress down the beach. Then he slows to pop open a final Molson. He realizes he shouldn't have spoken to Harrison about his observations. He's the employee. Harry is the client. Noelle is none of his business. Martin dreads the evening's outcome, wanting no part of anyone's marital bliss.

Harrison

Harry shuffles past Noelle, who is lying on the beach. She glistens with sweat and taps her left fingers in beat to the music plugged into her ears. Harry announces in a loud voice, "I'm back," as he lands upon the first wooden step toward the house.

Noelle jumps in recognition of his voice and swipes away her headphones. "Huh? Oh hi, Harrison. You guys are back?" Rising to her elbows, she sees Martin land upon the beach. "Did you catch anything?" She directs this toward Martin, rather than Harry who stands beside her.

"Nah, we were skunked," dismisses Martin. "Hey, you guys can hang out here for a bit. I'll bring the cooler up to the cabin. While I am there I will make some calls. Let's go shooting tonight." Marty drags the launch onto its wooden easel next to the other aluminum boats and heads up to the cabin. Instead of staying on the beach with Noelle like Martin suggested, Harry follows him inside.

Marty sets the cooler on the kitchen counter and enters his room as he dials his cell. Harry walks into the guest room, opens his dresser for his bathing suit, and overhears Martin's call. It is Elena, not the neighbor's lodge where they are going to shoot clays.

"Darling," Martin tries to sound jovial, yet Elena isn't having it.

"You break my heart, Marty."

"Why?" Martin sighs, preparing himself for what is to come.

"I have to do this and you know it," states Elena.

"You have to do what?"

"I have to have this child. Why can't we create our own family? Create our own dream."

Martin knows he and Elena make a handsome couple, yet plenty of handsome young couples break up. This is no small thing, and he isn't sure that his dream is the same as Elena's. "Listen, I can't do anything from up here. I don't want to make any promises over the phone."

"Can't you forgive our love for creating this child?" Elena softly weeps.

"I'd like it better if you didn't use that word. There is no need to use it," retorts Martin.

"What do you mean? Which word shouldn't I be using? Forgive, love, or child? Because each has the possibility to exist, Martin. Our child exists. It is forming."

"It's all wrong. It wasn't supposed to happen this way, Elena."

Defensively, Elena turns the conversation in a completely different direction. "Fine then. Couldn't you be good to me and let me go? If you don't want this, and I do, then end it."

"What do you mean, Elena?"

"If you won't come back with me, then let me go. I am going to have this child, and I am going home to Detroit. You know where I will be."

Stunned, Martin powers down his phone. Had his decade-long relationship with Elena just ended over a five-minute phone call?

Harrison lingers at the door with his trunks on and towel in hand. "Sorry to overhear. Lady troubles, Marty? I am going for a swim. Want to join us on the beach when you are ready?"

Martin nods numbly in reply. Harrison walks out the screen door toward his wife. Noelle, oblivious to the men's shared turmoil, hums to her plugged-in music, and lies immersed in her own world of problems.

Noelle feels the thud of Harrison's towel land beside her and looks up as her husband wades into the water. He gasps in reaction to the cold.

"Just get it over with Harrison. Dive in. When you prolong it, it's worse."

Harry breathes deeply and plunges into the cobalt streamlining out into the bay. He reaches a depth just over his own height. Tiptoeing on the sandy bottom, his mouth barely breaks the surface.

Harrison takes a deep breath and sinks toward the sand floor. He holds his ankles with his hands, his knees under his chin, and lets the gravity take him to the cold bottom. From the dark blue, Harry peers toward the surface, watching his air bubbles. He follows them upward, back to his reality, and breaststrokes into shore.

Dripping as he strolls out of the water, Harrison yanks his towel beside Noelle. The terrycloth trickles grains of sand onto Noelle. She scowls. Unaware of Noelle's reaction, Harry keeps walking and lets the screen door clang behind him as he steps into the cabin. Martin hears Harrison's entrance and announces that he connected with the neighbors at the old Mather Lodge.

"Hey Harry, shout down to Noelle. Tell her to come up and shower. We're going to head over to the neighbors to grill out. They said we can use their skeet launcher."

"Okay, who are these guys?"

"Randall and Andy, are a construction crew of two. The men volunteer for Michigan Historical Contractors. It's an organization that refurbishes historical sites often within National Park Service Land. The two are in college at Northern Michigan University studying Construction Management. They volunteer with MHC for the summer. It's one of their practicums."

"Oh yah? We will have to ask them about Northern then too," says Noelle as she emerges from behind the screen porch door with a towel wrapped around her body. "While you guys get ready, I can put together some food. I think there are burger patties and portobello caps in the refrigerator that we can grill."

Wet-headed from his shower, Martin collects the cooler and adds ice from the freezer. He loads the container with loose cans of Founders All Day IPA and Molsons for the boys and wine coolers for Noelle. Noelle wrapped burger patties in cellophane and set a package of mushrooms on top. Martin closes the lid firmly, as Noelle asks, "Do you have a picnic basket or canvas bag for the buns? I think we have a bag of Lays potato chips around here somewhere, too."

Martin hands her a reusable Meijer Supermarket bag to place the items. "Sorry, but you're going to be the odd lady out. Like me, this is Randall and Andy's last week on the island. So tonight's goodbye bash will be high on testosterone."

"Don't worry, Marty. I'm used to it. I'm outnumbered at home with Harrison, Mathias, and Malachi. It's part of the program."

Harrison blocks the doorway of the kitchen as Noelle skirts by to go change into clean clothes. "Do we need anything from the liquor cabinet? If not, I'm good to go."

Martin nods. "We're all set. Andy and Randall have a fine collection of tequila. I brought a few beers and wine coolers. They'll have other things to imbibe if you are so inclined." Harrison wheels the cooler out the door. Noelle emerges from their room to shoulder the grocery bag, and Martin starts the ATV engine to drive them across the island.

It would take a solid half hour to motor over to Mather Bay. The cabin, the Michigan Historical Contractors rented for the two volunteers, neighbored the Mather Lodge, which was about five and half miles on a diagonal four-wheeler path from Trout Bay. The two-track led inland through a hardwood forest. Martin advised to wear hooded long-sleeved jackets knowing the mosquitos would be fierce.

Pulling past the Mather Lodge, Martin parks the ATV in front of Andy and Randall's summer abode. "Look at those two goof-balls. They already have a snootful," remarks Harrison. Randall stands, extending his arms in the air like the gestures for the song Y.M.C.A. He whoops a hello.

Andy steps off the porch to shake Marty's hand and eyes Noelle. "These are our guests, Noelle and Harrison Phillips. They're staying at the cabin until the end of the weekend." Martin's tone reminds Randall and Andy to behave.

Harry extends a handshake to Andy, and pushes Noelle forward with his hand on her lower back. "My wife, Noelle. Thanks for inviting us over, Andy. We hear this is your last week on the island too."

Randall replies from the porch, "Yah, we head back to mainland. We have just over two weeks before we need to move into our student housing and school starts up at Northern. Damn, I'm not ready yet."

"What can we get ya to drink? Sipping tequila, rot gut tequila and orange juice, or... did I mention we have tequila?" quips Andy.

"Oh boy, I see where this is going. Boys, let's fire up the grill because we need to get some food in those guts if we're going to last the night," counters Noelle. They all agree.

Noelle sets the bag of potato chips on the picnic table next to the grill. Andy palms the dishes and precariously balances the napkins and silverware on top. Harrison wheels the cooler to the picnic table bench, sits, and pulls out a cold can of beer. Randall, with a Patrón tequila bottle in one hand, clutches a set of four shot glasses in the other. He lines the glasses on the table, pours a shot into each one, and holds his aloft to make a toast. "To the end of season. To the end of an era. To the end. Bottoms up."

Noelle downs her glass. Harry declines as he already had a beer in hand. "Maybe later."

"That's some good stuff. You should be sipping that not slamming it," says Marty as he walks over to the charcoal grill. Setting coal briquettes inside, he pours a splash of lighter fluid on top, and strikes a match from the box in his shirt pocket. From the same pocket he pulls out a joint, "Any takers?" Noelle, Randall, and Andy semi-circle the grill as they wait their turn for the blunt to be passed around.

Harrison shakes his head in slight disbelief. He is partying with twenty-year-olds, kids only slightly older than his eldest son. Mathias, who in his junior year of high school was getting caught, and in trouble, for the same thing his wife was inhaling across the yard. But, they were on vacation and he thought, "We all need to loosen up, now and again."

The hamburgers and portobellos were necessary sustenance. They all needed something in their bellies to mellow out the pot, the tequila, and beers. With a satiated belly, Martin notices the evening light dimming into dusk. He wants to target shoot before it becomes too dark. So, he asks Randall to set up the launcher, and retrieves the three-shot automatic loading 12-gauge from the ATV. "Randall, do you have target loads for a 12-gauge?"

"Yah, no problem. I have them inside. I'll be right back," replies Andy.

Harry follows Andy inside the house, asking, "Where's the loo?" and Andy points to the bathroom door.

"I'm just about to head in there myself. Help yourself to what's on the counter if you want some," invites Andy. "It's the end of the season. Gotta celebrate. You know what I mean?" Laying across the sink is a mirror, its usual place above the toilet looked oddly blank with a naked peg nailed in the wall. On the mirror, three lines of coke and a blunt razor blade await the next partaker. Harry hadn't taken a line since his college party days. Bending down, blocking his left nostril with his left fingers, he inhales with his right. The rush stuns him. He blinks, coughs, and clutches the door frame.

After the dizzy spell, Harry walks out of the door. He rounds the corner to where the others are looking out over Mather Bay. He sniffs and wipes the leftover snot from under his nose. Randall understands what that means, and hands Noelle the newly loaded shotgun tip up. "I'll be back. I'm going to help myself," he comments to no one in particular.

Andy announces, "Old dude is cool as hell, Marty. Where'd you find him? I never thought I would party like that with someone my dad's age." Noelle scrunches her eyebrows at Harry, not comprehending Andy's statement.

"Don't mind him. Tweedle Dee and Tweedle Dum are at it again and they have included Harry in their dumb-ass-ery." Noelle shrugs at Martin's comment, still not understanding. Instead, she releases the safety. "Okay, when you say pull Noelle, I'll let the skeet launch. On your mark."

Noelle lifts the gun to her shoulder and readies her right index finger on the housing. She looks down the barrel, and over the water where the sun hovers on the western horizon. "Pull." Martin releases the clays, and she blasts off two consecutively. Noelle lowers the weapon, leaving one shell in the chamber.

"No frickin' way. Mamacita's got game," stammers Andy.

"Never doubt the matriarch, Tweedle Dee," rebukes Noelle. Martin smiles at her sass.

After Martin, Harrison, and Noelle each have another round on the launcher, Marty announces it's time to head home. Harry, Andy, and Randall were still jacked up from their bathroom experiment, and probably would be up into the wee hours of the morning. Yet both Martin and Noelle, mellowed from the pot, are ready to call it a night.

Noelle grabs the vacant supermarket bag. Martin empties the cooler of the remaining ice. Harrison chooses the rear seat of the ATV and taunts in his intoxication, "Why don't you let Noelle drive back? Honey, show 'em what you got."

"Can I drive the ATV? Is it okay with the Outfitter?" Noelle tentatively asks. Martin figures they all had been doing plenty that the owners would not have condoned that evening. However, it was too late now. The damage done.

"As Harrison says, hammer it down, Noelle. Just turn the headlights on before you go."

Martin flips the lights for her, and she spins out of the driveway in reverse. Noelle heads down the dirt road, taking it a bit too fast on the curves. Once they are on the diagonal shortcut to Trout Bay, Noelle's navigation becomes trickier. The ruts in the dirt road bounce the ATV like a rollercoaster. A recent rainstorm had created rivets within the tracks, and what was easily passable in a slower gear and during daylight becomes precarious as Noelle is egged on to go faster and faster by Harrison's sporadic whoops.

Following a bend in the road, Noelle eases off the gas. Martin pats her right thigh indicating to go even slower. Noelle, high on adrenaline and the evening's imbibement, wishes Marty's hand would linger. She surprises herself, and pines for his forbidden touch, as tingles dart down her thigh. This spark reminds her of what it was first like with Harrison. Something that she hasn't felt in far too long.

Noelle is jolted out of her fantasy by Harry's pleas.

"Come on, woman. The mosquitos are fierce. Get me home!" Harry's insistence breaks her imagination and brings her back to reality just in time.

As the path straightened, a Mama Doe and her spotted fawn appear at the side of the road. Noelle slams the brakes and the ATV rear end fishtails right, nearly launching Harrison into the woods. The deer bound away, disappearing into the dark as Noelle slides the vehicle into park.

"Whoaaa, nelly. Women drivers. Marty, you can't take 'em anywhere."

"Honestly, Harrison. Shut your mouth. We almost hit a deer. Martin, take over. I have had enough criticism for the evening, thank you."

As the threesome make their way back to the cabin, silence presides over the vehicle. A quarter hour later, Martin parks the ATV. Harry stumbles off and leaves the cooler behind. Martin walks to the other side, and extends his hand with chivalry to help Noelle out of the vehicle.

Noelle holds Martin's hand a little too long. He caresses the inside of her palm with his thumb. She looks into his eyes, and exhales.

"Thanks, Marty. Good night. See you in the morning." Noelle makes her way up the steps, through the cabin door, down the hall, and into the guest bedroom.

Harrison waits behind the open door. When Noelle steps into the room, he closes it behind her and grabs her by the waist. She faces him, and Harry pushes on her hips, making her sit and lean back onto the queen-sized bed. She knows what is coming, and rather than say no, rather than delay the outcome, Noelle kicks off her tennis shoes as Harrison unzips her jeans. He tugs the ankles of her pant legs. Her jeans come off and pile on the floor.

Noelle inches her underwear off but Harry wants the naughty pleasure of the elastic tightening around his cock.

He imagines this as a stolen encounter with a co-ed Andy and Randall's age. A quickie on a dorm room couch. Harrison edges aside Noelle's panties, slides himself into her warmth, and rests his hand on her right clavicle. He's in a three-point stance, like in football. He's wound up and waiting for the quarterback's count.

However, at Harry's age, and without the help of his blue pills, things aren't coming like he thinks they should. Harrison tells Noelle to, "stay there and lay there." Predictable Harry, it is always and only about him. Noelle does as she's commanded. Immobilized until his thrusting stops; Harrison comes, and lays panting on top of her.

With tears leaking from the corners of her eyes, Noelle rolls Harry off her. In her disgust, she remains silent. She is tired of his treatment. She wants casual caresses that give her the tingles, not to be fucked and told not to move for fear of getting Harrison off his rhythm.

Harry rolls to his side. His North Face zip-away pants dangle awkwardly at his ankles. He shrugs them off and wipes himself clean with his boxers. Noelle leaves him on the bed naked, to go sit, dripping on the toilet. Taking a warm wash-cloth, she washes away the evidence of Harrison on her body. When she returns to the guest bedroom, and pulls on her pajamas, Harry sprawls atop the covers, passed out from his escapades.

A Day to Go

Noelle

At forty-two, Noelle is acutely aware that she does not
want to be alone. Yet alone she feels in her marriage to
Harrison. The steps by which she had acquired him, and
the way in which she had finally fallen in love, were all
part of a regular progression. She was young, and he was
a handsome older man. He had been married before, and
with Noelle, he had erased away what remained of his old
hurt. Children came quickly. Perhaps too quickly, and that
is what cemented them together. They had traded their
whimsy for security. Their desire was replaced by comfort
and the need to create the façade of a happy couple. But
clearly, neither was happy, not at all.

Noelle's bitterness seems to manifest in a physical fog.
It is morning, and her body aches from yesterday's liquid
courage and Harry's antics. Caffeine will give her the jolt
she needs. So rolls out of bed to start the morning coffee.
Filling the pot at the sink, she peers through the kitchen
window, into the woods where a bird feeder stands senti-
nel. A fluttering of chickadees, cardinals, and blue jays
peck at their breakfast.

And then, it came with a rush; not as a rush of water nor of wind, but a sudden odd emptiness. Noelle knew she had the answers that their "Divorce-moon" had set to provide. The summer's end on Grand Island had worked surprisingly efficiently.

The question was what to do next and how to do so with dignity. Noelle wondered how she should ride out the rest of their vacation on Grand Island. Was she settling if she kept quiet? Was she manipulative if she bided her time? The more she waited, the greater the emotional distance she created, and the further clarity she gained.

Meanwhile, an immediate remedy to her weighted thoughts appeared as she saw Martin round the corner of the cabin holding two mountain bikes by the fork at the base of the handlebars. Marty was nearly ten years younger; not only did he look at life with a youthful perspective, but his physique showed it too. As his sinewy arms clutched the bikes with control, she wondered how her body would feel embraced by those limbs.

Harrison disturbed her thoughts as he harrumphed and sat at the dining room table. "I'm not sure if I'm up for that mountain bike ride after all."

As planned, Marty had called the pay station on the mainland to rent bikes for Harry and Noelle. He had gone to William's Landing with the ATV that morning to pick them up. The rentals had been sent over on the morning ferry and awaited Martin at the interpretive center until he could haul them overland to the cabin.

Harry had recovered from knee surgery the previous winter, so in theory he was receptive to the idea. At least, he was when they first planned the bike ride. Now, Harrison sits at the dining room table, a topographic map of the island and the xeroxed visitor trail guide before him. He winces at the maps while sipping his steaming coffee cup.

"You need some aspirin or something stronger?" asks Noelle.

"I'm a bit hung. Maybe a little hair of the dog will wipe this dull numb away." Harry shuffles to the liquor armoire, and unscrews the Mount Gay rum. He pours a quick pull and adds cream to his coffee. "An 'adult coffee' to set things straight," he announces.

Marty comes in from the porch, his eyes meet Noelle's as she rolls hers in exasperation. "I went to William's Landing this morning and picked up the mountain bikes. They're outside resting against the side of the cabin. You have them for the day. Here, let me show you two on the maps what route I think you should do."

"You show Harrison, he's better at directions anyway. I will listen to you both from the kitchen while I make sandwiches for a picnic."

"Okay, knowing you need a picnic stop helps me figure your route. From here at Little Duck, go toward the Driftwood campsite. Take the hiking and biking only trail up to the Trout Bay Overlook. This will be a good spot for a picnic. To get there, it's a little over two miles. Harry, you saw the platform from the beach yesterday when we were in the row boat."

"Is it a climb?"

"Come on Harrison, you can do it. Enough griping. Are you worried about your knee? Why did you have surgery if you are just going to sit on your duff all the time?" asks Noelle from the kitchen.

"It's a bit of a climb. Just get off your bike and walk when you need. Take your time there. Have a nice lunch.

When you are ready to continue, take the trail toward the center of the island," encourages Martin.

"It sounds like it will be a great view. We need to make sure to take a phone with us, Harrison, so we can take some pictures."

"From the center of the island you have two options. You can take the road north up to the Mather Lodge, and say one last goodbye to Andy and Randall," smirks Martin.

"Nah, no need for sorrowful goodbyes. Besides, that will make the ride longer. What's the other option, Marty?" asks Noelle.

"You guys could go down the internal road past the Farm Field, which is the quicker route, or you can go out to Juniper Flats Group Site. There's an overlook of the west bay, and then you can take the four-wheeler road back along the coast down to William's Landing."

"I like the coast trail, Harrison. Let's do that. How long of a ride would that option be?"

"From the cabin to Trout Bay Overlook is almost 2 miles. From the picnic spot to the center road is 1.3 miles. From there to Juniper Flats is another 1.3 miles. Back down to the landing is about 3 miles, so that would be roughly 8 miles total. Once you are back at the landing, you should drop off the bikes at the ferry so the guys can take them back to the pay station. When you are at the ferry dock, you can flag down the Visitor Interpretive shuttle. The chauffeur will drive you to our four-wheeler road at Little Duck. By the time you're back, I'll have dinner prepped and ready to go."

Noelle peers through the kitchen door, "Sounds like a plan to me. Harrison, are you game?"

"I suppose," Harry says, making his way to the bathroom. Noelle and Martin hear him pillaging the medicine cabinet for aspirin.

When Harry emerges from the bathroom, Noelle is dressed in her biking shorts, tennis shoes, and tank top. Slung over her shoulder is Martin's borrowed CamelBak with chocolate peanut butter Clif Bars and sandwiches inside. "Come on, let's get going," urges Noelle, wearing a white bike helmet strapped to her head.

"If you think I am going to wear a helmet, you are crazy."

"Suit yourself, but get motoring. The longer we wait, the more humid it will be."

"Okay, okay. What am I going to even wear? I don't have bike shorts and my khaki cotton shorts will give me swamp ass."

"Well, if you didn't bring running shorts, wear your bathing suit. Use your wicking t-shirt because it's breathable. Wear your sunglasses so you have something protecting your eyes if one of us kicks up gravel. I will wait for you outside. Fill up a water bottle before you head out. I am okay for water. I have the internal dromedary in this backpack."

Noelle slowly circles the cabin, again and again, practicing the gear shifting while Harrison gathers his clothes. "All set." Harry walks out, letting the screen door slam behind him. Sliding a water bottle into the holder, he straddles the bike. "Where to my queen?" he asks, following Noelle down the path along the campsites and up toward Trout Bay Overlook.

Noelle cruises on the two-track. Intermittently, she whoops excitedly. Her competitiveness guides her forward and she refuses to get off the bike, preferring to crank down into an easier gear to slowly surge up the trail. Harrison had given up long ago, and lurches off his bike to walk. They both finally reach the landing where steps further the ascent. They lean their bikes against trees and make their way individually up the precipice.

Noelle upends the CamelBak contents onto a picnic table. She places one sandwich in front of the other like plates, and the Clif Bars to the side as the utensils. She feels like a little girl, setting up a make-believe dinner, pretending to nibble on plastic food pieces, and drinking daintily from plastic tea cups. Her memory quickly vanishes as Harrison huffs and puffs into the clearing. Wiping his sweaty brow, Harry sits on the side of the bench looking into the woods, rather than out over the water.

"If you want to look out at the bay you can come and sit on this side of the bench with me."

"I'm good where I am" Harrison pants. "And that was only two miles? We have another six to go? Dammit."

Noelle bites into her sandwich as a response.

Harry chomps into his BLT. "Oh man, this is the best ever. Light on the bacon and mayo, but pretty dang good none-the-less."

Noelle nods in agreement and takes a swig of water from the CamelBak. "Martin's backpack is cool, no? I think I want to get one of these for hiking or trail running when I get home."

"I think you just think anything Marty does is cool," retorts Harry.

"Oh, knock it off. Are you jealous?"

"I mean, I notice. You think he's cool. I think you like him."

"Whatever. I'm married to you. If anything, you have a boy crush on him. You are trying for some boy-bonding conspiracy every time you make a snide comment about me to him. It's like you're trying to win him on your side. Well, Harrison, it isn't about sides."

"Then tell me Noelle, oh wise one. What is it all about? Has the Universe divulged anything new to you that you can bestow upon us?"

"Nice, real nice. Well, to remind you, we are here to concentrate on each other. The therapist said..."

"The therapist said, the therapist said. Enough of that. We both know where this is going, don't we." Harry gobbles his sandwich and pockets his Clif Bar for later. Without a further word, he rises and his long strides take him down the stairs to his bike waiting against the tree. Harrison starts on the trail leading toward the center of the island without his wife.

Noelle watches Harrison retreat and refrains from immediately following. Instead, she pauses at the overlook to scan the water. "Well, if this isn't romantic," she says begrudgingly.

By the time Noelle catches up to Harrison on the trail, she is too late to have seen what happened, but could guess by the aftermath. The trail took a steep decline, and like the diagonal four-wheeler road connecting the Mather Lodge road to the center of the island, this portion of the road was rutted and made for poor navigation.

Harry had spun out, much like they all had the night before on the ATV. Yet, unlike the solid tread of the four-wheeler which righted them, Harrison misjudged. The brakes wheezed, he skidded, and he up over ended on the gravel path.

Noelle finds him, lying on his back. Gravel embedded in his right palm, which he used to brace his landing. Harrison's bathing suit pulls revealingly, lodged in his groin, exposing flesh sweating blood like the droplets on a chilled white wine glass.

"Are you kidding me, Harrison?" Noelle yells as she slows her bike. Lowering it to the ground, she walks to her husband's side. "Seriously, what contest are you trying to win? The biggest dumbass?"

"Thanks for your concern," he moans. "I nearly break my fucking neck. Scrape the hell out of my leg, and this is the love you extend."

"Quit mansplaining. Let's get you on your feet."

"T' hell if I'm going to take that long route. We already had one romantic overlook. I can pass on another. We're going back the shortest route possible, and we're taking the shuttle all the way back. The chauffeur can bitch all he wants, but he is taking me door to door."

Noelle knows she will never hear the end of it unless she agrees to Harrison's pain laden demands. She rights his bike and takes it for a loop down the path to make sure the wheel holds true. It did, and she steadies it by the fork at the handlebars as he straddles it. Harry pouts like their youngest child, Malachi, when he scrapes his knees. "Like father, like son," thinks Noelle.

Martin

Martin knows he is playing with fire. The casual glances over the dining room table, the touch of hand as they both grab the cream to pour in their morning coffees.

For God's sake, she is ten years older and a high paying customer's wife. But he knows none of them are happy and it is his last summer hurrah.

Once Harry recluses to bed, bruised and sore; Martin scribbles a note to Noelle. Tucking it into the corner of the medicine cabinet mirror, he knows she will see it as she prepares for bed. Marty retreats to the beach, the Pendleton blanket tucked under his arm, and the neck of his guitar grasped firmly in hand.

> Hey N,
>
> Want to come out to the beach? We might see the late summer meteor shower or, if we're lucky the Northern Lights. Come join me.
>
> M

As Harry lies in bed reading his Jim Harrison novel; Noelle readies herself in the bathroom. Toothbrush in mouth, she mumbles Martin's note aloud. Does she dare go out on the beach to look at the evening stars with a man disquieted by his lover's demands? Is she trading one resentful man for another? Both of them are emotionally bruised. Could they keep their flirtations in check?

Noelle quietly walks into the guest bedroom, Harry pays no attention to her. He is lost in his book. Choosing to let him fester alone with his stinging wounds, Noelle slides her Athleta warm-up bottoms over her lithe legs and tugs on a long-sleeved t-shirt. She looks beyond the curtain into the dark, and sees the glow of a bonfire and hears the first strums of an acoustic guitar.

Martin sits cross-legged by the fire on the Pendleton blanket. He nods at Noelle as she rounds the fire and sits to his right. He continues playing the song.

Marty's tenor tells about a teacher calling the parent of a troubled child. The boy has been acting out on the playground, using his fists instead of his words. Noelle reflects on her own kids, Mathias and Malachi. Mathias will head to college soon, but is completely unprepared. As a typical teenager, his most recent acting out was through experimentation. He had been caught smoking pot while sleeping over at a friend's house. On the other hand, Malachi, is a bit younger and lets his angst out on the soccer field. Like the song, both boys are perceptive to emotional changes going on in the household. However, the changes don't entirely make sense to them.

Yet Noelle knows why, and the song answers it for her. "Sometimes moms and dads fall out of love. Sometimes two houses are better than one." Martin's voice sings that there is no one to blame, but Noelle casts blame. Harrison's coldness and patriarchal ways stifle her. However, she knows she has changed too. She is different than she used to be. She has become more open to what the Universe has been telling her.

Like the song, her intentions are good, but they aren't enough. She wonders if Mathias and Malachi will grow to understand. Is her love sufficient, or will they resent her decisions?

Noelle lets Martin finish the song before she says anything. When he sets his guitar down, he notices Noelle bend to wipe the sides of her face atop either shoulder. The lyrics had brought tears, which she is trying hide. "Holy shit," she exclaims with a sniffle.

"Amazing lyrics, no?"

"Marty, who sings it? I haven't heard it before."

"It's 'When You Love Someone' by James Taylor-Watts. He's a British singer-songwriter."

"Those words. They seem like what I should be saying to my kids. Malachi and Mathias are so angry lately. They aren't dumb. They see how Harrison and I treat each other."

"So, you haven't talked to them?"

"No, we both pretend like they are too little to comprehend. But I know, as they see all of this, they are learning. They are learning that this is the way to treat a woman. They will treat their partners in a similar way in the future. That is what I am teaching my children, by choosing to stay."

"That's pretty perceptive. Maybe that is one of the reasons why I am not ready to start a family with Elena. I'm afraid of what kind of dad I would be."

"Everyone worries what kind of parent they are going to be, Marty. That's part of being a conscious adult. We all wonder if we are going to turn into our parents, good or bad."

Martin shoves his guitar to his left side and extends his hand over Noelle's. She sits with her legs extended, ankles crossed, and the soles of her feet raised toward the fire. Her arms are drawn behind her, hands planted, and finger-tips forward to stretch the backside of her forearms. She glances down at his hand. They both recline, their backs gently prickled by the Pendleton wool. Noelle streamlines her arms above her head, lacing her fingers, and pointing her index fingers toward the dune grass. Marty rolls on his right side. He places his left hand on her sternum. He holds her, feeling the side of her body against his. Her sweet smell: deodorant, peppermint from her toothpaste, the pheromones. She leans into his hovering frame.

"It's a bit dangerous to bring a blanket down by a romantic fire and gaze into the stars with a man who isn't my husband."

They tempt each other. Lying together, on the blanket, in each other's arms. His nose touches her clavicle and sniffs along her neck toward her ear. "You smell like something sweet." Martin notices himself stiffening. Edging closer, he lifts his leg over hers, his thigh presses against hers. She feels him growing and touches him. The fabric of his pants acts as a barrier between their skin.

Martin guides Noelle to turn on her side, afraid of where this will go if she faces him. Yet, she feels wonderful there spooning against the curve of his abdomen. His right hand tucks under her torso to cup her right breast. Traveling under her waistband, his left hand finds its way to her clitoris. Noelle groans, arches her back, and presses her ass against his hardened erection. He kisses her where her hairline meets her neck. Martin sucks on her earlobe and asks, "Is it good this way?"

He lowers his pants and presses his hardened cock between her legs. The softness of his skin plays with her labia. Noelle turns toward him, teasing his body. They kiss. Tongues, saliva, desperation. They stop to catch a breath, and are surprised at their urgency. Marty rises on his forearms above her. His elbows nudge her collar bones and he places his hands to cradle her head while his fingers twine in her hair. Noelle looks into his eyes. Her thighs tingle longing for more, but she hesitates.

Suddenly they both are conscious of the rough wool blanket below them. Martin exhales deeply, realizing this is far enough. If they do anything further, there will be permanent consequences. They both understand that the moment is over.

Marty stands to rights his pants. He glances at Noelle and extends his arm. She thinks he will caress her head as he bends down. Instead, Martin grabs his guitar by the neck. Without a further word, he walks through the dune grass, up the wooden stairs, and into the cabin. Noelle leans back on the sand, straightens her clothing, and looks into the sky searching for answers.

Harrison

Harry's pain keeps him awake. While Martin and Noelle are on the beach, Harrison relocates from the guest bedroom to sit on the living room couch. With a half full tumbler in hand, he stares into the shadows of the room.

Martin walks into the cabin. It is dark yet Harrison reads an intensity emitted from Martin's body language. Marty doesn't see Harry in the shadows as he sets his guitar on the dining room table. He continues to the kitchen, turns the lights on, and cleans the last bit of dishes left to soak in the sink from their meal.

Harrison limps from the living room to the porch of the log cabin. Looking out over Trout Bay, the Milky Way streaks the night sky. Fireflies erratically light up the gently blowing dune grass. Although it is a beautiful evening, Harry's body throbs as his scabs harden and a yellow-blue bruise discolors his leg from kneecap to hip. Harrison self-medicates. He takes another sip of Mount Gay, leaving barely a drop left in the bottom.

"Damned island. Damn Noelle's 'transformative ideas.' The only thing that transformed is my leg, and into a scabby mess. What is she expecting anyway? A transformation of our marriage within one weekend? Fuck the counselor. Screw Noelle's manipulations. I'm fed up with this nonsense."

Noelle walks onto the porch. "The night sky is beautiful here."

"Of course it is. How can something like that be ugly?"

"Why do you *always* have to be so argumentative? I don't want to fight. Can't you just stop?"

"I am not *ALWAYS* arguing. Beside, when we fight, that makes the time pass."

"Harry, that's mean-spirited to say."

"But it's true," he retorts.

"Maybe we can up our exit ferry to get you off the island. I know our reservation is for the noon ferry, but if your leg is hurting you so much, maybe we can try for earlier. I will have Marty call it in."

Harrison sits on the porch couch. He looks beyond the wavering dune grass, out over the bay where the whitecaps pick up with the evening breeze.

"There's a breeze coming up."

"Noelle, you say the most obvious things all the time."

"I am merely trying to make conversation as you pout over your snifter glass. Grow up, it's a bad scrape. The kids get them all the time. Put some Neosporin on it. Take some Advil. Suck it up. Take the pain. If you continue to look at the Universe negatively, it will come back to bite you.... Next time, in the ass rather than on the leg."

"Ha, ha... You give a damn about so many things that I could give two shits about."

Noelle lifts his glass, swishing the remaining liquid. "Drown your sorrows in this. It seems to work every time." And retreats back to their bedroom.

Baring the Truth

Noelle

Noelle tosses and turns throughout the night. Harrison occupies three-fourths of the bed, sprawled out in his discomfort. Noelle tires of trying to balance herself on the strip of mattress closest to the edge. Instead of rolling off onto the floor, she relocates to the porch couch.

Noelle gazes out over the bay. The day awakens with the emerging green glow of the sun above the blue horizon. Noelle wonders if, like the sunrise, she is awakening into more than just a new day. Perhaps this is a new period; maybe she is transitioning into another epoch of her life.

Was she not hearing what the Universe was delivering? Marty's serenade, 'When You Love Someone,' was a crystal clear message. Sometimes it's better to have two households and not one. Sometimes moms and dads fall out of love. Sometimes the separation is better than being together. What was she not seeing?

Harrison's behavior demonstrates he has had enough as well. He uses substances to mask his emotions. He vocalizes his feelings through snide comments or explosive exasperation. His lost loving behavior is replaced with aggressive sex. Noelle reminds herself that rape happens in marriage, too.

What could be her miracle? Or is the "Divorce-moon" it? Did she need to wait for that ultimate sign, or were these subtle ones enough for her to do what she felt inclined to do? All she knows is that she does not want to make a rash move. Instead, she'll wait for the Universe to create that moment of clarity, because she pleads it to do so for her.

Martin

Marty hears Noelle rummaging about the cabin. It is early, really early. But he knows she has risen because she bumped into the door jam and muffled an expletive on her way to the bathroom. It is their last morning on the island and the ferry can come none-to-soon. They have nearly three hours before the arrival of the first ferry just past nine that morning.

Martin walks from his room, through the living room, and on to the porch where Noelle is seated looking out into the bay. Fog is burning off over the water. "Noelle, do you guys want to get the 9 a.m. ferry back to mainland or keep your noon reservation?"

"We can play it by ear. I'm sure Harrison will want to go and tend his wounds in his own bed, but he is comatose to the world right now."

"No, not comatose." Harry emerges from the guest bedroom, disheveled hair pointing north, and baggy flannel pajama bottoms hovering under his love handles.

"Well, since you guys are both up. How about we take the ATV to go huckleberry picking? We can grab a Ziploc baggy full and then come back to make our farewell breakfast feast of pancakes and bacon," offers Martin.

Despite Harry's limp, he is game for one last excursion if it means huckleberry pancakes. Noelle agrees and walks into the kitchen. She takes a to-go mug from the cupboard, fills it from the pre-set coffee maker, and finds the stash of Ziploc bags for their spoils.

Martin grabs the over-under 12-gauge and the automatic-loader shotgun from the gun locker. He loads them with buckshot because target loads would only piss off a black bear rather than do any damage. Martin hands Noelle the shotguns. "Hold on to these, please. You never know what animals might be foraging in the wee hours of the morning with us." She lays them on her lap, barrels pointing outward.

Martin starts the engine and they peel away from the cabin down the four-wheeler road. As they open out into the straightaway, Harry points to the right. "Bear scat," he says. It is about human-size but smooshed from a fat mountain bike tire. Martin slows to notice the dung peppered with berry seeds. He looks down at the flattened scat and remarks about the bear prints.

"You can see on the side of the road where the bear passed." With broken stems, the green foliage had turned mottle as it dried. The three came to an opening in the white pines, the early morning sun shadowed in a glade of low lying huckleberry bushes. The small plants seem adorned with tiny blue Christmas tree lights because the berries were so thick. They glisten in the dew.

Harry lopes from the ATV, favoring his scraped leg. He

bends with his Ziploc bag to pick from one section of the bushes. One handful of berries for the bag, one for his mouth. Noelle lingers behind the ATV, she cradles the automatic-loader in her left arm as she plucks indigo nuggets into her mouth with her right. Marty stands alone next to the ATV, the over-under rests on the back seat of the vehicle while he leans down to pluck a handful of berries. "These are good."

Twenty meters to Noelle's right, a crash of branches emits from the woods. Noelle seems mesmerized as she peers into the undergrowth and a bear cub emerges. She extends her right arm as if to pet it. The cub stalls in its tracks as Martin yells, "Bear. Mama bear. Harrison, get out of the way."

Just then, Noelle turns toward her husband to see the protective Mama stand on her two hind legs ten feet from Harrison's unsuspecting back. Noelle steps forward. She raises the 12-gauge, lowers it to her right shoulder, aims, and fires.

The buckshot pellets spatter. Harrison is struck in the left shoulder. Spinning, he drops his bag of berries and thuds to the ground in painful disbelief. The rest of the pellets go wide.

"Noelle, keep shooting. Shoot the bear," Martin screams. She releases another round as Martin grabs the over-under from the ATV. He pumps once and blasts the Mama in the chest. Both he and Noelle, empty their guns into the heaving black bear crumpled on the forest floor. In her death stretch, a claw extends toward Harrison's heel.

The bangs of the successive gunshots frighten off the cub. It bounds through the shaded woods away from the noise. Harrison lies on his stomach, having fallen first to his knees, then on his face. Martin reaches him and rolls him on his back. Noelle inches her way to flank Harry's other side. She is beside herself, sobbing tears of anguish. Although she is crying, she looks off into the brush, searching for a view of the cub. She is not crying tenderly over Harrison's contorted expression. Martin wonders if Noelle cries because she regrets that her aim was not more true.

Martin feels for Harry's carotid artery. "His pulse is strong and he is breathing." Harrison moans in pain as Martin lifts him to the vehicle. "Noelle, you are going to have to drive the ATV back to the cabin. I will hold Harry so he doesn't fall off." Martin sets Harry across his lap, like a large overgrown Golden Retriever. "Get on with it, Noelle! Come over here, put the guns in the back. Start the engine. We need to call for help."

Noelle follows Martin's orders numbly, crying all the while. "She was so beautiful. We killed her. What's going to become of her baby? Marty, what did we do?" Noelle drives from the scene of their crime. The black bear crumples in a heated pile, all dignity, all majesty, all the beauty trickling away in the blood pooling on the dirt below her body.

Harrison

They drag Harrison back to the log cabin and place him on the screen porch couch. He overhears them bickering back and forth about what to do next. Marty dials his cell phone and notifies the county EMS that Mr. Phillips has been shot. They discuss if it would be better to come over with the pontoon ferry and then ATV it to the cabin through the hardwood forest. Or, if a quicker route would be a sea-plane to Trout Bay and evacuate him from the beach.

Harry croaks in pain, "Can't you let a man die as comfortably as he can?"

Noelle, through her tears, clamors, "You're not going to die. You can't die if you don't give up." She holds Harrison's hand to reassure him as she kneels at his side, yet her words sound remote. What is coming out of her mouth doesn't seem authentic. It seems like an obligation, not what she really means to say.

Martin hangs up the phone and looks out into the bay. "There's a breeze coming up. It will make it difficult for the plane to come in to shore without grounding. I'm going outside to raise the emergency flag on the pole. That way, the pilot has a visual on the direction of the wind."

As Martin heads outside, Noelle asks, "Harrison, do you want a drink? I know you shouldn't. I know it is bad for you and will thin out your blood so you will bleed more heavily. But, the Mount Gay is the only real pain killer we have." Noelle enters the kitchen for a glass and retrieves the bottle from the armoire, finding less than a thimble left.

She hands it to Harry, and after taking the last swig he says to her, "Lars, the fucker. What a place, this Grand Island. I wish we'd never come." Harrison's truth was finally admitted.

"Don't blame Lars. He didn't shoot you. He only suggested this place to us."

"I am well aware of the fact that you are the one who shot me."

"I'm sorry, Harrison."

"Are you?"

"What do you mean?"

"Love is a pile of shit and I am the one who has crawled to shout from the top. You made me come on this crazy 'Divorce-moon'. You got what you wanted, an end to us. Just file when we get home."

"Do you think that this is fun for me? I know you are in extreme pain, but why do you have to turn into an ass-hole right now?"

"I don't want to leave anything unsaid. Want another shot at me? I'm sure there are more bullets somewhere around here."

"Nice. Real nice, Harrison."

Coldly Harrison responds, "What? Let's say it plain. I don't want to leave any loose ends. Let's shut this thing down." Harry drifts out of consciousness on the blood soaked couch.

Noelle glares at her husband. Without his ability to acknowledge her words she replies, "You don't have to de-stroy me. Do you?" and walks back into the kitchen.

Martin returns from the beach. The flag is hoisted and it tacks back and forth with the gusts of wind. Noelle leans on the door-frame, the door swings wide welcoming Mar-tin into the screen porch door.

"How long do you think before EMS will arrive?"

"I'm not sure. If it were calm, the sea-plane would be here by now. But the gusts are south by southwest, which will blow them out into the bay. It will be difficult for them to hover until we can get him aboard."

Harry's eyes flutter as he tries to follow their conver-sation.

Noelle notices him struggle. "What is it, Harrison? Do you feel strange?"

Martin bends down to test the pulse of Harry's left wrist. "His pulse is weaker than before and the coloring in his face is chalky white."

"How little do they know," Harrison thinks. For all the intuition Noelle claims she has, she isn't willing to see what is before her. Or maybe she is in denial, unable to accept that she is the one who pulled the trigger.

The hum of a plane drifting over the eastern cliffs and dropping into the bay echoes upon the beach. Martin and Noelle jog out to wave from the dune grass so that the pilot heads the plane in front of the cabin. An EMT opens the hatch and jumps into the shallows. A second crouches at the open door, guiding out a stretcher to the EMT in knee deep water. The second has a First Aid backpack strapped on as she slides into the water behind her partner. Martin joins them in the water to help lift the stretcher. Noelle opens the screen door to the porch.

The EMT with the First Aid backpack sets it on the ground. She unzips it and pulls out a stethoscope and a handheld flashlight. She raises Harry's sleeve, exposing his wrist to check his pulse with her thumb. At the same time, she puts the stethoscope to Harrison's jugular to listen. She can't hear her patient breathing. She lifts his eyelids and flashes the light to check his pupils. Nothing. She puts her hand on his chest, as if in a blessing, to see if it will rise and fall. Her hand remains still.

A strange noise exits Noelle, a deep guttural cry. "Harr-i-son. Plea-se." And he is gone.

Departures

Noelle

After Harrison's body was evacuated, Martin and Noelle rode the ATV to the pontoon ferry dock, where two officers greeted them. They had to abandon the contents in the cabin, as it was a crime scene under investigation. The two officers explained they would be taken to Marquette County Sheriff's Department nearly an hour away in Marquette, rather than the local Munising station. The sheriff needed to ask questions and determine that Harrison's death was not foul play.

As Marty and Noelle wait for the two squad cars to drive them separately, they stare at one another, unsure if they are allowed to talk, but choose to take the risk.

"Listen, Noelle, this flirtation thing we had, it meant nothing."

"Don't worry, Marty. I understand you want to run far away from all of this craziness."

"It was an accident, Noelle. It was an awful accident. All of it, coming here for your holiday. Me doing this last client trip. Our connection. And, what happened this morning. It's all one big fucking catastrophic accident."

"Was it really that horrible? Somehow I feel that the Universe had us collide together. You, me, Harrison, Elena."

"Don't mention Elena. She is innocent. Leave her out of it."

Noelle realizes she has overstepped once again. Fearfully, she eyes Martin. "What are you going to say to the officers?"

"The truth. It was an accident, a horrible, horrible accident."

"Can you forgive me, Marty?"

"You want to make peace? Noelle, there is nothing to forgive. Tell yourself, it was an accident."

"You mean keep this secret. Keep everything secret, always. Never tell them anything."

"I think you are carrying the symbolism of this weekend a little too far, Noelle. Or do I misjudge you?"

"Alright, Marty, alright. But, can I call you in Detroit... to let you know how I am?"

"This is it. We are finished here."

This, they both knew, was their start of never telling. Neither would express what truly happened, because whether it was a horrible accident or a regrettable intention, it happened and it was finished.

Martin

Martin sits silently in the interrogation room at the Marquette County Sheriff's Department. He wonders if Noelle is in the sound proof room beside him, or if she has been released.

A detective walks in and sits down in front of Marty with a folder of information. His tone is neutral, but Martin is sure it's the officer's "I mean business tone" that he had developed after so many years on the force.

"Well, I have looked over your written testimony. Your story corroborates with Mrs. Phillips's version. An accident. An awful accident. Is that how you want it to go down, Mr. Rouge?"

"Yes. Noelle, um, I mean Mrs. Phillips accidently shot him."

"Is that the real truth? Ya say there. You know. A few years ago, we had a case where a newlywed pushed his wife off one of the cliffs at Pictured Rocks. His first version was that it was an accident too."

"No sir, it was an accident all the way around," Martin states with conviction.

"Well, this is what we know. The EMTs flew the deceased from the island. An ambulance triaged the body to the Munising Memorial Hospital. From Munising, Mr. Phillips was medivac-ed to Marquette General Hospital for further query. The official documentation lists his cause of death as a heart attack due to wounds caused by blunt trauma."

"A heart attack?"

"It was compounded. The shot in the shoulder, the loss of blood, and the overall trauma induced massive cardiac arrest. Not to mention all the booze, and... the cocaine found in his system. You know anything about that, eh?"

"Grand Island Outfitters caters to a wealthy clientele. Like Vegas, what happens on Grand Island stays on the island."

"Hmm, I suppose. So what are your plans? You know

you need to stick around here a while until we officially confirm the evidence."

"I will stay here as long as I am needed, sir. I have an apartment in Marquette. My plan was to close down shop for the outfitter. But you are right. Although I have been living here for a while now, I think it's time to go home. Home to Detroit."

Elena

It has been two weeks since Marty arrived in Midtown Detroit. Elena had found a studio apartment in one of the old Victorian brown houses off Cass Avenue. She was studying for her next Sommelier Level and working at a nearby Spanish tapas restaurant.

Martin and Elena were back in their old neighborhood, from their undergraduate days. Elena didn't see their return as a failure. Midtown was resurging.

Elena reassured Martin that she would be there for him. He could try for a GA position in the Department of English at Wayne State. He could finish his comps for his M.F.A. remotely. With his diploma in hand from Northern, he would have a terminal degree, and then could apply for an instructor position at WSU.

The two of them had all of these things aligned, but Marty remained closed-lipped to what actually had happened. Elena only knows what the Detroit Free Press and the NBC Channel 4 news had covered. Both stated basic facts about the tragedy, but nothing more.

Elena waits for Martin to reveal what happened. It is doubtful he will ever confide.

Lying in bed after her shift at the restaurant, Marty spoons her. He smells her sweat, the garlic, and her subtle perfume. His hand cups her growing belly. "I can't form words about how I feel, about any of it."

"You mean you won't, Marty."

Martin responds more emphatically, "I can't, Elena. That's all that I mean."

"Have it your own way, Marty."

"That's what I mean. I don't have it my own way. None of it is. I wish to God I did."

Elena's voice quivers as tears well. "Don't you believe that I love you? Don't you think the things we've had and done should make any difference?"

"Elena, I don't even understand everything that happened. I don't want to talk about it. Let's just focus on the fact that I am back. I am a different man after what happened."

"Prove that you are different. Prove that you want to have this child with me. Listen, Martin, I am in this for good. We are having a baby *and* I am here for you. Both. Equally."

Martin observes her in silence. He notices the way her mouth curves. He gazes at her eyes. He wonders if their child will have her features. Would its personality be like hers or would it be questioning, like his?

Trying to reassure her, he whispers, "You're too good to me." Mentally, Martin questions if that is true or if he says this because he knows Elena wants to believe.

Book Club Guided Questions
for *Stay North*

1. Jim Harrison is quoted in the preface of *Stay North*. It is a quote that grounds Harrison. It establishes a scene and thrusts this novella into a place-based genre. Have you ever had a connection like this with a particular place?

2. Elena comes from the tight knit-community of Mexicantown in Southwest Detroit. Similarly, Elena wants to create her own community, in this case, a nuclear family. Why is the concept of origin and establishing roots important? Why does it seemingly terrify Martin?

3. Martin hopes to be an established writer one day. This is his motivation, to experience life at the fullest and to give his perspective on it to an audience. How are the women in this story the audience he craves?

4. Harrison Phillips III is a typical man's man, a la Ernest Hemingway or Jim Harrison. Yet, like Hemingway and Harrison's patriarchal characters, Harry also is flawed. Despite his masks, he is vulnerable. Discuss.

5. Randall and Andy are characters whom, for one night, provide comic relief within the others' tenuous relationships. Their comedic ignorance, as the naughty boys of summer, charms their fellow partygoers. It reminds the others of their youth, a time they no longer inhabit. Explain.

6. Noelle's character is defined by temptation. Temptation for all that she wants, all that life has proven short of giving, all that she hopes the Universe will provide. Reflect upon this concept. Can our temptations be fulfilled, tamed, and conquered?

7. Noelle grieves for the mother bear and the future of her cub. Does she see a similar outcome for herself? Is that why she is tearful?

8. The end of *Stay North* touches on the idea of regret and acquiescence. Is that where the characters are headed?

9. Both Noelle and Marty strive for their own versions of "freedom." Due to their choices, have they attained that freedom, or have they created their own psychological prisons?

Acknowledgements

Thanks to:
Daniel Combs, my husband, partner and constructive critic. To our adventures.

To my first readers:
Brian Stephenson, who has witnessed the evolution of this project. Larry Thompson, a friend from college, a brother in this journey, and an adviser on outside living in the Upper Peninsula.

To the various Writers' Retreats at Interlochen Arts Academy that I have attended:

Mardi Jo Link's guidance on how to access one's vulnerability. Katey Schultz's insight as to how to set a scene and advance plot through action. Patty McNair for how to build characters through humor and tragedy. Desiree Cooper who demonstrates that strong women protagonists can command action through their subtlety. As well as to other participants in these workshops who shared their work: Marcus Trammel, T.J. Harrison, and Julia Poole. Thank you for building a creative writerly community.

To the editors and designers at Atmosphere Press:
Your expertise has helped me get this story out there.

And lastly, thanks to the place itself. Grand Island, north of Munising, ever watching over the Pictured Rocks National Lakeshore. Like Jim Harrison's quote from *Sundog*, it is one of my places in nature that has its own unique spirit. Its peculiar draw, acts as a magnet of contemplation within the beauty of nature. Humanity needs places like these.

We need to preserve our wild spaces.

About Atmosphere Press

Atmosphere Press is an independent, full-service publisher for excellent books in all genres and for all audiences. Learn more about what we do at atmospherepress.com.

We encourage you to check out some of Atmosphere's latest releases, which are available at Amazon.com and via order from your local bookstore:

Relatively Painless, short stories by Dylan Brody
Nate's New Age, a novel by Michael Hanson
The Size of the Moon, a novel by E.J. Michaels
The Red Castle, a novel by Noah Verhoeff
American Genes, a novel by Kirby Nielsen
Newer Testaments, a novel by Philip Brunetti
All Things in Time, a novella by Sue Buyer
Hobson's Mischief, a novel by Caitlin Decatur
The Black-Marketer's Daughter, a novel by Suman Mallick
The Farthing Quest, a novel by Casey Bruce
This Side of Babylon, a novel by James Stoia
Within the Gray, a novel by Jenna Ashlyn
Where No Man Pursueth, a novel by Micheal E. Jimerson
Here's Waldo, a novel by Nick Olson
Tales of Little Egypt, a historical novel by James Gilbert
For a Better Life, a novel by Julia Reid Galosy
The Hidden Life, a novel by Robert Castle
Big Beasts, a novel by Patrick Scott
Alvarado, a novel by John W. Horton III